## "Nick, I ca

Danielle—the woman, the woman he'd just been thinking about—materialized at his side. He'd imagined her in his bed, her head on his pillow. But the reality of her standing beside him now was far more potent than any fantasy. His eyes swept over her, stopping at the gap of bare skin below the T-shirt she wore.

"I wanted to thank you again," she whispered. "Because of you, I can let my guard down."

He forced his gaze up, past that bare tantalizing belly. He shouldn't be thinking these thoughts. She needed his help, not his overactive libido.

She hesitated, then continued boldly. "I want what we should have had all those years ago."

Her words stunned him. Did she mean what he thought she meant?

She tugged at the light blanket he'd thrown over himself. Her gaze roamed over him, greedily taking in his naked chest. His breath caught at the heat that smoldered between them.

"I want this night, with you. Make love to me, Nick."

Dear Reader,

I hope you've enjoyed reading about the Rhode Island branch of the Cooper family. I'm grateful to the COOPER'S CORNER continuity for letting me live out fantasies that have no place in my reality. Being on the run, for instance. In my life? No, thank you.

But in *For the Love of Nick,* it works. Danielle Douglass is on the run from the law, with only her one-hundred-pound puppy and her wits to guide her. Thankfully she runs into one particular sexy memory from her past—Nick Cooper.

Tall, dark and slightly attitude-ridden, Nick is the answer to her prayers...and her greatest nightmare, because Nick wants to show her what's missing in her life.

I hope you enjoy this prequel to the continuity series COOPER'S CORNER. Look for my upcoming Duets titles in October—*A Royal Mess* and *Her Knight To Remember.*

Happy reading!

Jill Shalvis

## Books by Jill Shalvis

### HARLEQUIN TEMPTATION

### HARLEQUIN DUETS

### SILHOUETTE INTIMATE MOMENTS

# Jill Shalvis
# FOR THE LOVE OF NICK

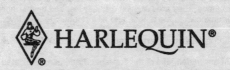

## HARLEQUIN®

TORONTO • NEW YORK • LONDON
AMSTERDAM • PARIS • SYDNEY • HAMBURG
STOCKHOLM • ATHENS • TOKYO • MILAN • MADRID
PRAGUE • WARSAW • BUDAPEST • AUCKLAND

ISBN 0-373-25985-9

FOR THE LOVE OF NICK

Copyright © 2002 by Harlequin Books S.A.

Jill Shalvis is acknowledged as the author of this work.

# _____Prologue_____

AS IF SHE HADN'T just broken the law, Danielle made a full stop at the red light before getting on the highway heading back toward Providence. "Well." She glanced at her passenger. "It's official, you know. We're on the run. Outlaws."

Sadie didn't answer; she was too busy enjoying the breeze from the open window.

"At least the car isn't stolen," Danielle said. "But we have to have it back to Emma tomorrow." She let out a laugh that sounded slightly more hysterical than humorous, and checked the rearview mirror for flashing lights. "I wonder if they'll let us share a prison cell."

Sadie pulled her humongous head back inside and craned her thick neck toward Danielle. Her tongue hung out as she panted her hopeful agreement.

Danielle sighed at her best friend and loyal one-year-old bullmastiff, a dog she'd raised with her boyfriend.

Ex-boyfriend.

Ex-*psychotic*-boyfriend.

Luckily Sadie wasn't psychotic. Just unsure of men.

That made two of them.

Danielle checked her rearview mirror again, grateful to see nothing but light traffic and the bright colors of spring in the Rhode Island countryside.

Apparently, she'd truly gotten away with it. Stealing Sadie back. She had simply pulled up to Ted's house—where he'd had Sadie staked on the lawn in the sun without water—and released the grateful dog, who'd been nearly beside herself at the sight of Danielle. "I wish you could talk," she said, checking her rear mirror yet again. "Or hug. I could really use a hug."

Sadie stopped panting and looked at Danielle with her heart in her eyes. As if Danielle was her hero.

"Stop that." She glared out the windshield. "I'm not a hero." Her gut twisted. If she had been, she'd have been smart enough to see this coming. Strong enough to protect Sadie.

She'd almost been too late. As it was the poor dog had been underfed in the time Ted had kept them separated. And given the heart-wrenching way Sadie was hanging on Danielle's every movement, she'd been neglected entirely. It was a crime, as Sadie was just a baby, really, albeit a one-hundred-fifty-pound one.

Okay, more like a brick of brawn than a baby, with a broad, well-padded head set on a thirty-four-inch neck sturdy as oak. But she was adorable, and she was Danielle's. Well, half, anyway.

She had no idea how she could even put a roof over their heads, now that Ted had changed the locks on the house, stolen her car and emptied her checking account.

The police hadn't had time for the case. First of all, the house was Ted's, leaving her with little legal recourse. Second, Ted had bought her the car he'd taken back.

The money though, that had been all hers, hard earned from her job as a professional dog handler. Not that she had legal recourse there, either, as she'd actually given Ted the PIN number for her bank card.

Danielle could handle her stupidity in letting herself get ripped off, but living with the fact she'd nearly lost Sadie to a man who could, and would, hurt her had been untenable.

Sadie, restricted by the seat belt across her body, leaned on Danielle. Hard. Her hug.

The lump in Danielle's throat was more from lingering stress than anything, but comfort was comfort. "Thank you," she said, smiling when Sadie licked her from chin to cheekbone.

But even the superfluous slobber of a lovable bullmastiff couldn't mask the facts. She was truly on the run. She, a woman who followed the rules and was honest to a T, reduced to common criminal status with nothing more than approximately forty-nine dollars in her backpack, her laptop and a tank of gas in the car she'd borrowed from her friend Emma. "But I couldn't have done anything different," she murmured to Sadie. Not when Ted's sudden and terrifying temper against the dog had become so clear.

How had she been so blind for so long?

But she knew the answer to that. Ted had been wealthy, intelligent, gorgeous...and interested in her, Danielle Douglass, a nobody from the wrong side of the tracks, with no father and a distant-hearted mother who'd had little to give her daughter.

In comparison, Ted had paid attention to her, he'd made her his world.

God, that hurt, that she'd been shallow enough to fall for a few good lines and a pretty smile. Only the smile hadn't lasted, as Ted gradually had reeled her in, absorbing her life into his, leaving her uncertain, unbalanced, and more alone than she'd ever been, despite the fact she'd been alone a lot.

His rage against Sadie had been the last straw.

Danielle knew he was reacting to the fact she loved the dog more than him, that his pride was hurt, and maybe also the fact Sadie had lost her last dog show, but it didn't matter.

She was out of his life. And God help her, so was Sadie.

She was so tired. The result of sleeping in the borrowed car for a week, using a friend's shower when she dared, biding her time until she could steal her own dog back.

Not that the law would see it that way, as Ted held all of Sadie's papers in his safe. With time and money, Danielle figured she could try to prove otherwise, that while they had shared physical custody of the dog, it had been *her* to provide the love and comfort.

But she had neither time nor money on her side. Ted wouldn't take lightly to her stealing Sadie from beneath his nose—never mind that he'd done the same thing first. Disappearing, and fast, was her best plan. If she only had a good professional photo of Sadie, she could go to Donald Wutherspoon, a reputable art director she'd been introduced to at a show a few months ago, and hopefully get Sadie a commercial endorsement.

That would mean money. Which would mean security. Stability. Two things Danielle most definitely needed in her life.

Determined, she got off the highway. First up, she bought two Big Macs, one for Sadie, one for her. Fortified, they found a phone, and two photograph studios listed in the Yellow Pages for Providence. Garnering some hope, she closed her eyes and blindly pointed to one.

"Wish me luck," she said to Sadie, and dialed.

# 1

THE PHONE RANG. And rang and rang. But as he was sprawled in a hammock soaking up the rays, with a drink nicely balanced on his belly, Nick Cooper pretended not to hear it.

It wasn't his fault his sisters had jumped ship and deserted their photography studio to chase after the men in their lives.

Okay, so they hadn't jumped ship. Kim had gotten married and deserved her honeymoon. Her twin Kate deserved a break, too, which was why she was at this very moment far away from Rhode Island, all the way in Hollywood with her new stuntman boyfriend.

And after all, they *had* asked if he minded. He just hadn't known how to tell those four melting, pleading, expressive eyes no.

The phone kept ringing.

"I'm not an answering service," he said into the delicious spring air, loath to move even an inch.

But he *was* an answering service. He'd looked

into his sisters' hopeful gazes and had caved like a cheap suitcase, promising to take messages and set appointments and make nice with whomever called.

Even if making nice was not his specialty.

"Okay, yeah, yeah. I'm coming." Hey, he was on vacation, too. Extended leave, actually, from his job as a news journalist. He had a great job, a Pulitzer prize and the freedom with which to travel the world over as he pleased.

Oh, and a monster case of burnout.

He supposed being called home to the States, to Rhode Island in particular, back to the so-called normal life to attend Kim's wedding had been a blessing in disguise. Somehow.

At least the relaxing part wasn't half bad.

"Hello," he said into the phone. "Providence Photography." He let out a silent sigh as he switched to work mode. "Can I help you?"

NOT TOO MUCH LATER, Nick heard the front door of the studio open. Hard to miss it with the ridiculously noisy wind chimes someone had attached to the thing. Probably Kim, who had a notion for such things.

Damn it, she was early. Whoever *she* was, the

woman who'd called, sounding harassed and harried, asking for a dog portrait.

Who the hell would waste good money on a dog portrait, of all things?

Coming off his recent trip reporting from South America, with some of the poorest regions in the world, such an extravagance seriously annoyed Nick.

But it wasn't his place to wonder about the woman and her strange request. He'd offered to set up an appointment for when his sisters returned. They were the experts, he was just answering phones like a good older brother.

And napping. Lots of napping.

But the woman had sounded panicked and desperate. She'd even, when he'd tried to get rid of her, resorted to begging. Hell, that had done him in but good; her soft, honeyed voice pleading as if her very life depended on it.

Nick's family had often accused him of having a save-the-world complex, and maybe that was partly true. But mostly, he figured, he had a woman complex.

He couldn't seem to resist them.

Seeing as that was the case, it was handy to be back, as he had dates coming out his ears for the remainder of his stay. He deserved a little casual, mutually satisfying playtime after all he'd seen and done in the name of journalism over the past years.

"Hello?" A woman's voice rang out.

Oh yeah. Definitely the woman from the phone, with the voice that could melt the Arctic. Damn, he was such a sucker.

*"Hello?"*

"I hear you," he called out. "Hang on a second." He stood in the darkroom with some film he'd shot in Belize only a few weeks before, just finishing up the developing. A hobby, not a profession, which explained how he'd nearly ruined the entire roll.

But he was glad he hadn't. Leaving South America for his sister's wedding, he'd been tired and exhausted, having just handled a particularly grisly story of murder and mayhem among two feuding drug lords. On the way to the airport, along the side of the road, he'd come across a group of children playing. Not as they played here in the States, with toys and gadgets and electronics. Not these kids, who'd probably never had a single possession to call their own in their entire lives.

They'd been playing at a game of stones, and

their sheer pleasure at being alive and free to play had grabbed him by the throat.

The picture was of a boy no more than six, half-naked with his ribs and stomach protruding. He held his treasured pile of stones, grinning a toothless grin, which made Nick smile, too.

"I appreciate your working me in like this," came the woman's voice again, just on the other side of the door now, removing his thoughts entirely from that world and placing them firmly in the present.

She still sounded soft and sweet, and more than a little harried. "No problem." He wondered if she had a face and body to go with that sensuous voice. Wondered if she was lush and curvy, or lean and petite. Wondered if she dressed as hot as she sounded. Wondered—

"Sadie is very cooperative."

Oh, yeah. She had a way of speaking that brought to mind sweaty, wild, against-the-wall sex. "Sadie?"

"My dog. She'll be no trouble at all."

Hell, he'd nearly forgotten. But how hard could it be to snap a photo of a dog? If he couldn't do that, then he ought to just pack it in and call it a day. "Be right with you."

Suddenly he was looking forward to this doggie gig. Sure, he'd had a nice, leisurely afternoon planned out, but Nick was nothing if not a man willing to make the most out of every opportunity. Spending time in the company of an incredible-sounding female seemed nice and leisurely, too, so he hung up the last picture from his roll, wiped off his hands and opened the darkroom door.

And was greeted by a sight that made him grin.

His pretty-sounding client had her back to him. Specifically her butt, as she was bent over a mass of something he assumed was a dog. Not a canine-lover, Nick ignored the animal and let his gaze soak up the very nice view its owner provided.

She wore khaki shorts that were riding up at the moment because of her bent-over position, and since he happened to be somewhat of a lingerie connoisseur, he could tell she wore thong panties, as nothing marred the clean lines of the shorts over the twin curves of her cheeks.

*Very nice,* he thought on an appreciative sigh. Her legs were nice, too, long and bare and toned. As for the rest of her, he caught a blur of equally nice long, toned arms in a white sleeveless blouse, and a flash of shoulder-length, wavy, russet hair as she whirled around with a half smile already in place.

*On her hauntingly familiar face.* He knew that face, knew that body. Knew those misty gray eyes. And one night, a lifetime ago, he'd known more than that. *"Danielle?"*

Her smile faded, replaced with an expression of shock. "My God. Nick. I haven't seen you since..."

"High school graduation." Never taking his eyes off her, Nick shook his head at the vision of all his adolescent fantasies, standing in the flesh before him. They'd gone through four years of school together, and though they'd never spoken except for that one fateful night, he'd had enough imagination even then that it hadn't mattered.

How many nights as a horny teenager had he lay in his bed, staring at the ceiling, thinking of the hottest girl in the school, knowing he wouldn't get a chance to be with her? He would have sworn that that girl had never, not once, noticed the tall, skinny nerd he'd been.

And yet she'd known his name.

That's when he heard the odd rumble, and realized there was a huge mass of teeth and muscle standing behind Danielle.

Growling. Not a friendly, how-do-you-do growl,

either, but a should-I-eat-your-face-or-your-heart-first sort of growl.

Nick had faced guerrilla warfare, crash landings in unfriendly territories, typhoid fever and countless other emergencies, but he'd never quite imagined himself going like this.

He took a better look at the dog, or what he hoped was a dog, as it was past hip height to Danielle. Its short muzzle was black, and at the top of this inky mask, two mahogany-brown eyes peered out below a thick, simian brow. The shorthaired coat was a riot of brown-and-black tiger stripes.

Yep, just a dog.

The next thing Nick knew, he'd been hit in the chest with what felt like a bowling ball. No, make that a *wrecking* ball. Staggering back, he hit the wall, but was saved from sliding gracelessly to the floor by the two huge, massive paws on his chest, pinning him in place.

Nick stared into the brown, bloodshot eyes and realized the dog was about as tall as he was. There was a huge tongue, lots of drool and really bad breath. That's about all he caught before Danielle lugged the thing off him.

"Sadie," she admonished. "You've got to stop greeting people like that."

Nick straightened and ran a hand down his shirt, grimacing when he encountered great globs of...slobber. *"Greeting?"*

"Well, she's a bit nearsighted. She likes to get close to see your face."

"Uh-huh." Nick glanced down at the biggest, beefiest dog he'd ever seen. "I thought she was interested in eating me."

"Oh, no! Sadie is the sweetest thing, she'd never hurt anyone." Proving so, she bent and cupped Sadie's huge jowls in her palms, smiling a smile that seemed both indulgent and infinitely sad. "She's had a rough time of late, that's all."

And so had Danielle, Nick guessed. He knew little about her other than she'd headlined his every wet dream for several happy years, but his instincts were never off. Something was wrong, he could see it in the exhaustion in her eyes, in the way she carried her lithe body. Hell, he could practically smell it on her.

And everything within him wanted to ask her about it. Could he help? He'd done so once, though he'd always wondered how things might have been different if she'd let him do more. It did startle him how easily and instantly he fell back into that pattern of wanting to save her.

But damn it, he was on vacation. No rescuing fair maidens in distress required. He was going to just hang out, take some pictures, get some recreational sex if he could, and do whatever came to him that didn't demand much thought.

And yet it was utterly beyond him to ignore anyone's problems. Just as he opened his mouth to ask her about it, she closed off her expression to his questing gaze. "So," she said. "Who's taking the pictures of Sadie?"

"You're looking at him."

"Oh. Can we get started? I'm a bit...strapped for time."

# 2

NICK EYED SADIE with a wariness that might have amused Danielle under any other circumstances, but this wasn't just a whim. And she really was strapped for time, even if she wanted to stop time and just stare.

Nick Cooper. God, she'd always wondered about him, wondered if... No. She couldn't go back. What was done was done.

"I don't suppose I can talk you into waiting," he said. "As I mentioned on the phone, my sisters—"

"No." As she half expected the cops to come haul her away, and as she hadn't yet proved ownership of Sadie, she had to press on. "I can't wait."

His eyes had always been amazing, almost hypnotic in their fathomless green, and now they landed on her, slowly assessing. Certainly kind, certainly compassionate, but she didn't need kind and compassionate, she needed those pictures.

"So why don't you tell me what's wrong?" he said after a long beat.

So he was still intuitive, still willing to put aside everything else and come to her aid. But she was no longer a lost, frightened, desperate seventeen-year-old. She didn't need his help, she needed his camera. "Nothing's wrong." To go along with her denial, she forced a smile.

He looked her over for another long, unsettling moment. As before, taking his sweet time. And as before, leaving her squirming because she had no idea what he saw when he looked at her like that.

But he simply nodded. "Okay, then."

Danielle followed him down the hall toward one of the studios, still oddly unnerved at the sight of him. Whatever he did with himself, it involved his tall, leanly muscular body, which looked like one fully honed muscle. He wore jeans, faded and soft-looking, though there didn't appear to be one single soft thing about him. They clung snugly to his backside and thighs, the fabric of his shirt stretched across his broad shoulders. She couldn't seem to tear her eyes off him.

While she was staring stupidly, wondering how the boy she'd known had grown up into this picture-perfect man, he happened to glance back, and caught her.

He smiled, a friendly, no-secret-meaning-attached-to-it smile, and it was so simple, so contagious, she almost smiled back.

Ridiculous as it seemed, this man wasn't just a blast from her past, but something else, something deeper, something she didn't want to face after everything else. He was dangerous to her mental well-being, and she instinctively knew it.

"I've wondered about you," he said. "About where you'd be, what you'd be doing."

While that made her tingle in even more awareness, she shrugged it off. "Nothing special, really."

"You had special written all over you," he said. "Still do."

She'd been on her own for...well, forever. She needed no one. Especially now, after Ted. So she couldn't possibly be looking into his timber-green eyes, suddenly yearning to throw herself against him and beg for help.

Just because her life had gone to hell in a hand-basket was no reason to fall apart at a familiar face. No reason at all. "I haven't thought about high school in a long time," she said.

"I try not to think about it at all."

She could believe it. By some grace of God, she'd been popular in those days. It had always baffled her. She'd been born on the wrong side of the tracks and had worked at a fast-food joint until all hours of the night helping her mother keep a roof over their heads. As a result, she hadn't had the best of grades, and yet she'd hung with the "in" crowd—at least on the days she'd been coherent enough to socialize and not falling over in exhaustion.

They hadn't always been the nicest of kids, her group, but for whatever reason they'd accepted her. But it still bothered her to think about how many others they'd taunted or been cruel to, for no good reason other than they could.

Nick had been one of those other kids.

She remembered him well. He'd been gorgeous even then, though back in those days he'd been tall, lanky to the point of skinny, and tough. Very tough. Way too much so for her crowd to try to break through his wall of resistance. They'd tormented him—not that he'd ever given an inch or even let them know he was bothered.

She herself had never done anything to him, but

it shamed her that she'd stood in the presence of kids who had—boys who'd tried picking a fight, girls who'd snubbed him.

Nick hadn't appeared to care, going on as if they hadn't existed. Until that one night when she'd needed him, and without question or rebuke, he'd been there.

Just as he was there for her now.

No doubt, he was a world removed from the boy he'd been. No longer did his shoulders look too wide, his chest too broad for the rest of his body, which had gone from too skinny to oh-just-right.

He'd turned out...spectacular. No other word need apply.

Not that she was noticing. God, no. Her head had been turned by an interesting face before and look at where that had landed her. No more men in her life, thank you very much, especially men who could melt earwax at fifty paces. She had other, pressing concerns.

Such as being on the run from the law.

Details.

But she was so engrossed in those details, and the fact that Nick quite possibly had the best set of buns she'd ever seen, that she didn't realize he'd stopped in front of an open studio until she plowed into him.

"Oops." Her hands automatically lifted to brace herself, setting down on his back. Snatching back her hands, she thrust them behind her. He'd been warm and rock-hard. "Sorry."

He didn't seem bothered in the least, the opposite actually, as he turned and gave her another smile.

"So..." She nearly stuttered. "What's first?"

"You bring in—" He gestured to the leash she held.

Sadie. Who stuck her head around Danielle's legs, looking as if she'd rather face ten Teds than be here. "Woof," the dog offered cautiously; a loud, low sound of nerves as she shifted back and forth on her massive paws.

Danielle coaxed her into the studio with a biscuit from her pocket while Nick moved in ahead of them to set up.

"Look," she whispered, squatting before the uneasy dog. "Do this for me. Do this for our future." She cupped Sadie's huge jowls and looked deep into her worried eyes. "Please?"

Sadie leaned close and licked her chin, and Danielle hugged her tight. "I know. You love me. I love you, too," she promised softly. "It'll be okay."

"What will?" asked Nick, who'd come up behind her.

# 3

"DANIELLE? What will be okay?"

Meeting Nick's steely, curious gaze, Danielle unwrapped her arms from around Sadie and stood. "The pictures," she said as smoothly as she could. "The pictures will be okay."

"Uh-huh." Nick studied her for another long moment, in that deeply personal, intense way he had, the one that told her he wasn't missing a thing.

Neither was she. She might have known this man when he'd been a boy, but that had been a very long time ago. She knew nothing about him now, and had no reason to trust him, even if she wanted to.

His eyes stayed on hers. "You need a backdrop. Outdoorsy or traditional?" Pulling down several, he gestured to her choices. "Personally, the traditional makes any subject look wan, but the outdoorsy one is fairly cheesy, so..." He lifted a broad shoulder. "I'm not a professional. Just pick the one that appeals."

He wasn't a professional. *So who are you?* she wanted to ask, but that would be getting to know him, that would be opening herself up, and she wouldn't do that. "You're not thrilled about doing this."

"I said I would."

His tone suggested he would always do what he said. But she knew that wasn't the case. People lied. People changed. People couldn't be trusted. She drew a deep breath. "The cheesy outdoorsy backdrop, please."

A small smile crossed his face as he pulled down the screen of a wooded clearing surrounded by pine trees, wild grass and a little creek. Definitely on the cheesy side.

But that smile...holy smokes, it should be registered as an illegal weapon. She watched his hands on the backdrop as he pulled it into place, mesmerized by the flex of the muscles in his forearms, by the easy, economical movement of his body as he straightened and looked at her.

"Warned you," he said, mistaking her unblinking stare for shock over the backdrop. "How do you want the dog?"

"Uh..." Danielle shook her head to clear it and concentrated on Sadie, who was looking at her with suspicious concern. "Standing at an angle to the camera to show off her coloring."

"Coloring?"

"Most of her breed is a solid shade of red or fawn. But Sadie's dark stripes are what the original English breeders had in mind when they crossed a mastiff with a bulldog. I'd like to show that off."

"Got it." He put his eye to the lens, fiddled with the camera. "So...what do you do these days?"

"I handle dogs."

He pulled back from the camera to look at her. "You mean for other people?"

"Yes."

"Are they all like that?" He gestured to Sadie, who was currently eyeing her tail as if she wanted to chase it.

"Bullmastiffs? Mostly."

"Why?"

"Why?" She looked at Sadie, wondering how anyone could not see her innate charm. "Well... They're big. I love big dogs. And they're short-coated, with unmussable fur. It makes it easy to get them ready for the ring. See her inherent facial makeup, with her black mask and kohl-like eye shadow?" She cupped Sadie's big face and kissed her nose. "Adorable, guaranteed. But also, there's no extra grooming required. She shows *au naturel*. The only tool I need is a towel for the drool."

"You mean a bucket," he noted, watching as two long lines of it came out of Sadie's mouth, puddling on the carpet.

Getting down on all fours next to Sadie, Danielle wiped the drool away and physically maneuvered the dog's paws where she needed them, getting the front two in place before crawling around the back, only to have Sadie sit. She then leaned into Danielle and licked her face.

Nick laughed.

Danielle ignored both the contagious sound of that good humor, how it made her tummy flutter, and tried again. Leaning forward, she shifted Sadie back into place. "There. Stay. Oh, perfect! Nick, quick."

Nick ducked behind the camera. Danielle, still on her hands and knees, quickly backed out of the way.

And...Sadie lay down.

Straightening from behind the camera, Nick shot Danielle a raised eyebrow.

Which she ignored. "You're not helping," she

whispered to Sadie, crawling forward so that she could look at Sadie nose-to-nose. "Now let's try that again—"

Behind her came a funny sound.

Whirling, she found Nick standing next to the tripod. Staring at her. Staring specifically at the butt she'd obliviously thrust into the air.

Oh good God. Face hot, she lowered her bottom to her heels. "Sorry."

"Don't be. Best pose I've seen all day."

Her gaze locked on to his and refused to be freed. More than her face felt warm now, her entire body ignited. Her skin seemed pulled too tight, and her nipples poked at her blouse. Feeling betrayed by her own body, she turned to Sadie, careful to be far more modest this time as she once again coaxed the dog into the right position.

Sadie held that position until exactly the second Nick reached for the flash, when she promptly walked right off the set and sat down at Danielle's feet.

Nick cocked his hip and studied Sadie. "Is she really some sort of champion?"

"She is." Danielle sighed when Sadie yawned again. "You're boring her."

"Maybe I should dance and sing."

"Just keep trying." Desperation was clawing at her. Could she get the shots developed right here and now? Or would he give her the film so she could try another lab?

It had to be one option or the other, as she had to go from here straight to Donald Wutherspoon, in the hopes he'd get work for Sadie.

And income for her.

If not, then she had to get another job, quick. She was qualified, and after ten years, quite reputable as a handler. People knew and trusted her with their animals and she'd made a decent living at showing champion dogs. But stealing a dog, even for a really good reason, would ruin her. Not to mention the fact that Ted would likely look for her at any local show, or even within all of Rhode Island, which just wasn't big enough for her to disappear.

Danielle couldn't let Sadie be taken back. If she could only earn enough cash to disappear, then she'd go far, far away and start over, doing whatever she had to in order to make a living to support the two of them.

"Hey." Nick suddenly appeared in front of her, cupping her jaw in his hand, looking deep into her eyes, making her realize he'd called her name several times. "What's really going on here?"

His fingers were on her skin, electrifying her. "What do you mean?"

"You're jumpy and nervous." His eyes were so deep, so tuned on her, she had to swallow, hard.

"Maybe I'm always nervous around strangers."

"We're not strangers."

No. No, they weren't. "Well, then maybe I'm nervous seeing you again."

"When you rarely gave me the time of day?" He let out a rough laugh. "Doubtful." His thumb stroked her jaw. "So tell me. What's really up?"

With no idea what she was going to say, Danielle opened her mouth, but before she could respond, Sadie nosed her way in between the two of them and bared her teeth at Nick.

Nick lifted his hand off Danielle. "A watchdog, are you?"

Danielle stroked a hand down the ruffled hair at Sadie's thick neck. "She won't bite."

Nick eyed the dog warily. "If you say so." But he didn't touch Danielle again.

Shouldn't have touched her in the first place because now he had the incredibly soft, satiny feel of her flesh implanted on his brain.

"If you'd pet her, maybe smile at her, she'd probably relax," Danielle suggested.

"If I pet you, smile at you, will *you* relax?"

Her eyes widened for a moment on his before she looked away. "You're playing with me."

"I don't play with people's feelings."

Her huge eyes met his. "Do you still hate me?"

*"Hate you?"*

"You know, from high school."

He stared at her for a moment, then laughed, but she didn't so much as smile, so his own slowly faded. "Danielle, back then, hating you was just about the furthest thing from my mind."

"Even after...that night?"

"Especially after that night."

When her misty eyes blinked in surprise, he nodded wryly. "Yeah. Big-time crush."

"I had no idea."

"No kidding."

She grimaced. "I'm sorry. I hate to think about those days, about the kids I hung with, and how mean they were—"

"It was a long time ago." He backed away from her, annoyed that he'd brought any of it up. Annoyed that he'd still occasionally wondered about her. "Like I said, I don't think about those days anymore."

She glanced down at Sadie, that vulnerability and infinite sadness back in her gaze. "Yeah."

Just looking at her again made him feel like that stupid, gawky teenager he thought he'd left behind years ago. *Had* left behind years ago. He was a successful, respected journalist. He had a life, a great one.

He didn't need this. He nodded toward Sadie, suddenly eager to see them leave, eager to get back to his carefully unplanned leisure time, where he didn't have to think or feel. "Let's just get your pictures, okay?"

"Yeah." Danielle tried to pull Sadie before the outdoor screen. Sadie didn't want to go. Digging her paws in, jaw stubborn, she held back.

But apparently Danielle was just as stubborn because she pulled and pulled with all her might. "You're…going…to pose," she grunted.

Fascinated and amused in spite of himself, Nick watched. Danielle's brow was furrowed, her hair in her eyes. Her face, tight with concentration, slowly turned as red as it had when she'd realized she'd shoved her very nicely curved bottom in his face.

Filled with determination, she did indeed eventually budge the dog, and he had to admire the strength in her willowy frame for doing so.

"You...could...help," she rasped, getting Sadie on the right spot, tossing him an irritated look that only made his grin wider.

"Why? You're doing great." The dog had to weigh over a hundred pounds. No way was he going to push it around and risk losing a finger or more. He was fond of his fingers. And fond, he discovered, of watching Danielle sweat.

He wondered what else would make her sweat and grunt like that. Wondered if she liked down-and-dirty sex, if she—

Whoa. Back the truck up. He was *not* having those thoughts, not about this woman.

"Okay," Danielle said breathlessly, straightening. "Get ready, Nick." She stroked the dog, soothed her, kissed her nose, even rubbed her cheek against Sadie's.

Nick watched this honest display of affection and felt something tug inside, good and hard. Damn it.

"Take the picture," Danielle said. "Quick."

Nick moved behind the camera, watching through the lens as Danielle praised and hugged

Sadie, with little disregard for the dog hair sticking to her clothing, for the drool that dripped down one arm, for her own wildly rioting hair, or the way she once again presented him with her delectable backside.

"Ready?" she tossed over her shoulder.

"Ready," Nick said, eyes glued to her body as she quickly moved out of range.

When the camera shutter closed, she sagged back against the wall in relief, closing her eyes, breathing deeply.

Mesmerized by the emotions crossing her fine features, Nick moved from behind the camera and came to stand before her. "It's just a picture."

Her eyes flew open. "When can I have them?"

"In about three weeks."

"How about I pay you for the film? You can just give me the roll and I'll get them developed myself."

"That's not the way Providence Photography works," he said, absorbing her growing panic. "Danielle—"

The bell above the front door of the studio chimed. Danielle jerked to face him. "I thought you said you were closed."

"We are." Nick groaned at the thought of taking

more pictures. Because bad as a dog was, it could get worse, far worse.

He could have to take a baby picture.

"Nick." Danielle gripped his shirt when he turned to go out front. "I need to tell you—"

"Hang on, I'll be right back." But short of prying her fingers from him, he couldn't budge her. Then he saw her face, which had gone colorless. "Hey." Concern replaced everything else, and without thinking, he stroked her hair from her face, touching her cheek. "What is it?"

"If it's the police—"

"The police?" He went very still. "Why would it be the police?"

"If it is," she repeated, swallowing hard. "I—"

"Hello?" called a male voice from out front. "Sergeant Anderson. Anyone here?"

# 4

"OH MY GOD." Danielle slapped a hand over her mouth. Her blood pounded in her ears as her heart dropped to her toes.

Sensing her distress, Sadie butted her big head into Danielle's stomach, knocking her back a few feet. She dropped to her knees and hugged the dog close. "Shh," she begged, pressing Sadie's broad face against her chest. "They won't take you back, I won't let them."

The promise was genuine, though she had no idea how to keep it. Above her, Nick swore under his breath, and she spared a second to feel incredibly stupid for getting into this situation. How had they found her?

And what would Nick do now? Turn her in?

Of course he would, anyone in his right mind would. He had no idea what was happening or what she'd done. No ties as distant as theirs were would warrant him getting in trouble with the law for her.

"I'll be right out," he called out to the waiting sergeant. He stared down at Danielle. "I'm in the darkroom, just give me another second."

Then he dropped down beside her, forcing her chin up. Odd, but his long, warm fingers on her throat were the most comforting thing she'd felt in a very long time. So was the way he looked at her, as if he was deeply concerned. As if she mattered.

His body was close, so close she could have moved a fraction of an inch and let him support her. Tempting. God, so tempting.

But that would be weak, and one thing Danielle refused to be was weak.

Nick brushed up against her. He put his mouth to her ear, eliciting a shiver at the feel of his breath fluttering her hair. "I take it you're in some deep shit?"

He smelled good, pure male, she thought inanely. His hair curled over his ear so that her breath disturbed the strands. He felt warm and solid, and she wanted to press closer.

Why was she noticing such things at a time like this?

"Danielle?"

"You...might say that I'm in a tad bit of trouble," she whispered.

"What's going on?"

"It's a long story." She didn't want to tell him how pathetic she'd been to have had her entire life taken away from her. Closing her eyes, she waited for him to call out and announce her presence. Any self-respecting citizen would.

"Did you hurt anyone?"

Her eyes flew open. "No!"

"Commit murder?"

"God, no!"

"Okay." He put his mouth to her ear again. "Whatever they think you *did* do, are you innocent?"

This time his lips touched the sensitive skin just beneath her ear, and another shiver wracked her frame. A shiver he must have taken for fear because he ran a hand down her arm.

"No," she managed, blinking up at him because he wasn't betraying her. Why wasn't he betraying her? "I'm not innocent. But I only did it to protect—"

"*Hello?*" the officer called out again, sounding unmistakably annoyed.

"Coming!" Nick looked at her for another long heartbeat before closing his eyes briefly, muttering something about being a damn, sentimental fool. "Where did you park your car?"

"It's not mine, it's my friend's. Down the street and around the corner. There wasn't any free parking out front and I didn't have change—"

"Thank God for small favors. Get in the closet. Sadie, too." He opened it, put those hands of his on her hips to guide her in.

"Wait." She resisted his hands when she really wanted to close her eyes and whimper at the feel of them on her. "I don't want to get you in trouble."

"I do fine in that area all on my own, thanks. Now get in."

"I don't need your help, Nick."

"I hate to argue, but it would appear you do. Again."

Yeah. Again. God, that burned. Especially when her pride was all she had left. For a moment, she almost wished he was a perfect stranger, that they had nothing in their past to give them this odd, inexplicable connection she didn't understand and didn't want. "I can do this myself."

"How? By running out the back door and hoping they don't hear you? Get in," he urged, pushing her in the closet. Leaning in after her, he squinted into the dark. "You okay in here for a few?"

That he would take the time to ask nearly broke her. But she gathered up every last dollop of inner strength she had and nodded as if she did this every day.

Nick turned to Sadie. "You too, dog." Apparently unwilling to push the dog in, he waited to be obeyed.

Drooling, Sadie studied the wall.

"Get in," he repeated, cautiously reaching out with his foot to gently shoo her in.

Sadie leapt as if he'd tried to kill her.

Nick looked as startled as the dog. "Hey, just get in the damn closet."

"Here," Danielle said quickly, pulling Sadie in herself, letting out an *oomph* as the nervous dog sat her considerable weight in Danielle's lap.

"Don't make any noise," Nick commanded in a hushed tone. And then he was gone.

Danielle sat there in the dark with her one-hundred-fifty-pound baby. In her life she'd been in some pretty tight and uncomfortable situations, but this...this definitely took the cake. "We'll be okay," she said softly.

Sadie turned in her lap, nearly breaking her legs

in the process, pressing her warm, wet nose into Danielle's neck. Four paws shifted up and down in nervous excitement, wondering when the games began.

"This isn't fun time," Danielle whispered. "Shh, now."

But Sadie was convinced it was a game, and got herself all wound up, which meant more drooling, more rustling, more frantic maneuvers on Danielle's part to calm down the young dog. "I know," she whispered, wrapping her arms around Sadie's bulky neck. "I know, I know. You want to play, but hang on."

Her legs were killing her, strained with the weight of the heavy, overgrown puppy, but there was little room to shift in the loaded closet. Still, she managed to lay back, scooting over to give Sadie enough room so that she could get off her lap.

Marginally better. She had no idea what she was stretched out over, but it was actually quite comfortable, soft and pliable, and she relaxed slightly.

Finally getting the message that it was quiet time, Sadie cuddled up beside her.

It was so dark. She could hear Nick's voice, could hear the policeman's voice, but couldn't make out the words. A wide yawn escaped her.

She had hardly slept in days, and she felt it now, in every ache of her body, in her fuzzy—and quickly getting fuzzier—thoughts.

*Don't fall asleep,* she told herself, though Sadie already had. Her deep, steady snores mocked Danielle's exhaustion.

Counting didn't help. Neither did thinking of the mess her life had become.

Nick. She'd think of Nick. He had a smile on him, a smile that went all the way to his eyes. Ted hadn't smiled like that, as if he really meant it.

Why had she never noticed that before?

Nick had a voice on him, too, she was listening to it now as he talked to the officer. In her not-too-distant past, she might have fallen for a voice and a smile like his, but not now. Falling meant trusting, and she just didn't have it in her to do that, not ever again.

"It'll be okay," she whispered to her sleeping dog. Somehow it would, and she curled up and closed her eyes.

SERGEANT ANDERSON EYED the photo studio reception area, his sharp eyes missing nothing, but thankfully, there was nothing to see.

Not out here anyway, Nick thought.

"You're certain you don't have anyone scheduled for today?" the officer asked yet again.

"As I mentioned, we're closed," Nick answered. "My sisters run the place, and they're on vacation for several weeks yet."

"You're not a photographer?"

"I'm a journalist."

"What if someone calls you, wants to book an appointment?"

"I'll book it."

Sergeant Anderson narrowed his eyes and watched him very carefully. "But you won't be opening for business?"

*Danielle, what have you done?* "Have you ever tried getting good pictures of a baby? Or a high school grad student?" He shuddered. "Nightmare waiting to happen."

Anderson slowly nodded, his gaze taking another slow tour of the place. "Yeah, I have one of those grad students. She's into makeup, boys, looking at herself in the mirror, and more boys."

"Exactly."

"So anyone wanting their picture taken is going to get turned away?"

Nick didn't look at the south wall, where at this very moment, on the other side, sat Danielle and her damn dog. If either of them made a noise, or so much as sneezed, they were all in very big trouble.

What the hell had gotten into him when he'd shoved her in there and had offered to help? Had he lost his mind?

Yes, he admitted. One look into her lovely but vulnerable eyes and he had indeed lost brain cells at an alarming rate.

And now, though it made no sense, he offered his first lie. "Turned away flat. So what's this about, anyway?"

Anderson took one last look around. "I'm looking for a woman who's going to want a professional photograph of a dog she's stolen. There's only two photograph studios in the immediate area, so..." He headed toward the door.

Nick walked him there, hoping that would be the end of it, but of course, nothing was ever simple.

Anderson had one last thing to say. "If a woman named Danielle Douglass comes in with a dog, here's my card. Call me."

Nick took the card, controlling his dread. "What will happen to her?"

"We'll worry about that."

After he'd shut the door, Nick leaned back

against it and drew in a deep breath. At heart, he was a journalist. He hunted out stories and told the truth. The whole truth and nothing but the truth.

There was a story here, a big one, only he didn't know the half of it.

He would though. He definitely would. Pushing away from the wall, he moved down the hallway, into the studio and opened the closet door.

He expected...well, he didn't really know exactly what he expected, but it wasn't the sight that greeted him.

Danielle had fallen asleep among a throng of stuffed animals his sisters used during photo shoots for kids.

But as the light fell on her, she sat straight up blinking sleepy eyes, looking dazed, rumpled and a little confused.

And sexy. Very sexy.

"Did you really fall asleep?" He refused to let his eyes soak in the very arousing sight of her lying stretched out over stuffed toys. She should have looked ridiculous, but instead, looked warm and...inviting, as though if he pressed in and joined her, she'd welcome him by leaning back and opening her arms. She'd wrap those bare arms and legs around him and—

"Was he looking for me?"

He looked into her eyes, the color of an approaching storm. "You know he was."

With her hair falling over her shoulders, she set aside the stuffed teddy bear she'd been hugging. "I couldn't hear what you were saying out there."

"It's hard to hear when you're asleep."

"I wasn't."

But she had been, and all he could think was, what kind of exhaustion could override being sought out by the police? "I think we should start at the beginning, Danielle."

"The beginning?"

"Is Sadie that rare?"

She followed his finger to the blissfully sleeping Sadie. "Yes."

"What makes her so?"

She stroked the dog. "She's called a 'typey' dog."

"Meaning?"

"Meaning, as I told you before, she shows all the characteristics of her breed to maximum effect. It's her coloring, it's as perfect as there's been in a hundred years. Her marking, the black outlining, the stripes? It's as the breed was originally intended. She wins shows on her appearance alone."

"Lots of money involved with that winning?"

"No." Her mouth twisted wryly. "Silly as it sounds to someone not in the business, it's not about the money. It's about prestige. Glory."

"Ah." Nick looked at Sadie and tried to imagine glory in running the dog around a ring filled with spectators and dog crap.

"Sadie has that prestige and glory, and she gives it to whoever has her."

Nick rubbed his temples. "So what's the story here? You haven't murdered anyone, or physically hurt anyone. We got that far."

Danielle climbed out of the closet. At the loss of her beloved master's body heat, Sadie lifted her head, yawning so widely it seemed she could swallow a man's head whole. Then, realizing she was alone in the closet, she scrambled to all fours, only to slip. Without breaking stride, she was up and trying again, her toenails scratching the floor as she clamored for purchase where there was none to be had.

"Slow down, sweetie," Danielle murmured, reaching out to stroke her massive head.

When the dog had finally freed herself, she leaned against Danielle, who staggered under the weight before bracing her legs farther apart.

Sadie rubbed her head against Danielle's belly, making Danielle smile at Nick sadly. "She loves me."

"I can see that." For a moment, a very brief moment, he wondered what it was like to be the object of such deep love and devotion. But then he imagined how much the dog must eat a day—and excrete—and shuddered.

He was not a dog owner and was quite satisfied with that.

Danielle patted Sadie's head. Her own hair was a mess, and she had a crease across one cheek where she'd lain her head on a teddy bear but as she leveled that somber smile on Nick, his heart simply stopped.

Then her smile slowly faded. "I stole Sadie. I co-owned her with a man. My boyfriend."

Nick didn't know which was more disturbing. The fact he'd lied to the police over a damn dog or that Danielle had a boyfriend.

Not that he should care one way or another. He had his own life, a good one. He even had hot dates lined up. Dates that wouldn't require thinking, wondering, dreaming or yearning.

Given that Danielle required all of that and more, he ought to show her the front door.

"When we broke up," she said, "Ted wanted Sadie."

*They'd broken up.*

"She's worth money," Danielle admitted. "But for Ted, it's all about the glory. She's a champion, and her bloodlines are incredible. He expected me to breed her, handle her descendants."

Nick shook his head. "This is a custody battle." He couldn't believe it. "Over a *dog?*"

"It's more than that, Nick."

"Obviously, or the cops wouldn't be out looking for you. So what did you do, steal her from him in the middle of the night? Did you also accidentally steal his cash and silver, too?"

Her eyes flashed. "I took Sadie and only Sadie. But I had a good reason."

This was bad. He'd gotten in the middle of some silly dog dispute. And why? Because he remembered her fondly from one night well over a decade before. Because he was an idiot. "So Ted saw her as investment property and you see her as your firstborn?"

"Worse." She looked as if she didn't have a friend in the world. She look as if she might cry at any second, and Nick let out a long breath, a complete sucker for a female in distress.

For *this* female in distress. He had no idea why just their brief, all-too-long-ago connection should still matter as much as it did. "I'm sorry," he said over his better sense, but she looked troubled, alone, and damn it, scared. No way could he turn from that. "Tell me the rest."

"I broke up with Ted when I could no longer ignore his possessiveness."

There was a note in her voice that got his full attention now. Sadie was sitting on her haunches at Danielle's feet, twin strands of drool coming from either side of her open mouth. She was panting, her tongue hanging out, watching Danielle with hero worship. Danielle put her hand on the dog's wide head and sighed. "It got ugly, and I discovered something else about him."

"He had a temper," Nick guessed, feeling sick.

When she slowly nodded her head, he stepped close, very gently putting a hand on her arm. "Danielle—"

"It started when Sadie lost a dog show. It was so hot that day, and quite frankly, she just got bored. Ted really wanted to win that one because his biggest competition was there watching, but yelling at her wasn't the answer. And then afterward Sadie limped, like her hip was bothering her. She was really skittish." She looked down at Sadie with defeat. "I think he kicked her."

"You think? Or you know?"

"I just know." Her voice wavered. "And then a week later she wouldn't get into her crate when he wanted and I caught him at it. I saw him kick her."

Nick looked into Sadie's dark, doggie eyes and tried to imagine anyone kicking a dog that came up to his hips and nearly outweighed him. Not that it mattered. Nick happened to hate violence with a passion, especially against the innocent, and as big as Sadie was, she was an innocent. In as calm a voice as he could manage, he asked, "And you? Were you being abused, too?"

She straightened. "He wouldn't dare."

Sounded like he dared, all right. It was more like the guy had never gotten the chance. Damn it, why him? Why here and now, with a woman he didn't seem to be able to turn his back on? With a woman he appeared to be more than willing to save yet again?

Ah, hell, who was he kidding. He couldn't have turned his back on *anyone.* That it was Danielle made it only worse.

"You can see why I can't let her get taken back,

right?" Danielle asked, determination in every line of her tense body. "I just can't."

"Okay." He shoved his fingers in his hair and tried to think. "Can you prove Sadie is yours?" She just bit her lower lip, making him groan. "You can't. Which is why you're on the run with her."

"I can prove we *shared* ownership, yes, but that's not good enough. They might make me share her, and I can't let that happen. I paid for half of her when she was a puppy, but that's not so easy to prove, it turns out, as there was some comingling of funds along the way between various vet bills and food and things." Bending down she hugged Sadie tight, and in return, the dog licked her ear.

Then Danielle looked up at Nick with those huge, huge eyes. "All I need are the professional shots of Sadie to give to an art director I know. He's going to get me some commercial endorsements."

"Which equals money."

"Yes."

"And you need the money to..."

"Vanish." She pressed her face into Sadie's neck. "Ted drained my bank account. With an ATM card I gave him."

He stared at her, saw her pain and humiliation,

and bit back his oath. "What about your family? Can't they help you?"

"It's just my mother. We're...not very close. Besides, she doesn't have any extra money."

"I see." And damn it, now he did. She was truly alone in this. She was going to take her dog and walk right out of his life.

He should let her.

But he didn't want her to go. Didn't want to lie awake for the next fifteen years still wondering *what if....*

# 5

"WELL." Danielle put on a smile that might have wobbled just a bit before she forced it, and reached for Sadie's leash. "I can't tell you how much I appreciate what you've done."

Nick was standing close, too close, looking edgy and more than a little unnerving because of it.

What did he want?

He'd let her in. He'd taken the pictures he hadn't wanted to. He'd put up with the nervous Sadie when he didn't know or understand dogs.

And he'd lied to the police.

That alone would have made her grateful forever, but now she owed him, and she hated that. Combined with all the memories from so long ago, with her silence over her friends' behavior, with the way he'd saved her that night as he had today, she felt unsteady. Nervous. Over the years, Nick had become the chance she had never—but should have—taken.

Now, on top of it, he'd touched some personal

part of her she'd promised no man could ever touch again. "Thank you," she said, knowing it wasn't enough.

His sharp green eyes narrowed, and he shoved his hands into the pockets of his jeans. "That sounds like goodbye."

"Do you suppose I could take the film you shot of Sadie? I'll pay you for it, and then have it developed myself."

"Where?"

"I'll take it to one of those one-hour places."

He winced.

"Oh, don't be a photo lab snob now," she said, trying not to notice how her body liked being close to his, how it leaned even closer, making her stomach tickle. How his hands were shoved low in his front pockets, drawing her attention to— "I really need to go," she said abruptly.

"Yeah." His hands came out of his pockets to touch her arms. He stroked them up and down the limbs she hadn't realized were chilled from stress and worry. And in spite of herself, she let out a little shiver that had nothing to do with being cold.

At the involuntary movement, he went still, very still, as if he felt it, too, that inexplicable connection from his flesh against hers.

An odd sound escaped her, one that sounded horrifyingly like...*need*, so she bit her lip to keep quiet.

In return, he let out a rough groan. "Do you remember that night, Danielle? The dance?"

She closed her eyes, her heart squeezing as the years fell away in her mind. "I remember." It played across the backs of her eyes with startling clarity. "Prom."

"You looked beautiful."

"I was with Adam Bennett."

"Star of the football team." His voice hardened. "First-class asshole."

Danielle opened her eyes, but the images were still there. "He took off, leaving me in the parking lot because I...um, didn't want to..."

"Yeah." Nick's eyes held so much, she could hardly look at him. "I gave you a ride home."

She'd stared out the passenger window of his car, wondering if all men were jerks. "You never said a word, didn't tell me how stupid I'd been to go with him, about how my friends treated you, nothing." She marveled at that all over again. "You just drove me home, to the trailer park I didn't want you to see, walked me to the door, and..."

A ghost of a smile crossed his mouth. "That *and* gave me great dreams for years."

He was staring at her mouth, making her stomach fizzle again. "It was just a kiss," she said.

"Hmm." His lips curved into a full smile now. "Some 'just a kiss.' You should know, I've never forgotten it."

"Me neither," she admitted. It hadn't been like her other experiences. He hadn't shoved his tongue down her throat or his hands up her shirt.

Nick's mouth had been gentle, tender and incredibly, amazingly arousing. If she was being honest, then she also had to admit she'd yearned for another like it. From him, something she'd been sure had been a lost opportunity.

They were nearly mouth to mouth now, and though she had no idea who'd moved closer to whom, she stood there staring up at him, mesmerized. He stared, too, for so long her tongue darted out to lick her suddenly dry lips.

With another deep, dark sound from his throat, he stepped back. "Damn it. I can't."

"Can't...what?"

"Can't let you walk out of here, knowing you're in trouble."

She couldn't remember the last time someone

had looked at her like that, as if she really mattered, and without warning, her throat closed. In danger of losing it, she sought to lighten the mood that had spiraled out of her control. "Do you save all the fair maidens?"

"Only you, apparently." He wasn't going to help her lighten anything. "Where will you go?"

"You don't really want to know."

"Yes, I do."

"If you don't know, we can go back to what we were. Two people who went to high school together, two people who've lost track of each other." She turned away. "You don't know anything about me, and—"

"And what?" He whipped her back to face him. "You don't know me? Here, try this. I'm business-sitting for my two sisters. I have a great family I don't see often enough. I'm a journalist. Hard news, mostly. I dabble in photography. Just took my first dog shots. The past two weeks have been my first vacation since..." He frowned. "Since I don't remember." His frown deepened. "What else do you want to know?"

"Nick—"

"I've been traveling the world writing stories since right after college, and you know what?" He bent a little to look right into her eyes. "I can't re-call when I've been back here for more than five days straight since high school graduation, and yet we ran into each other. Here. Now." He touched her jaw, shaking his head in wonder. "Don't you think that's odd? Or maybe just fate?"

"I don't believe in fate," she said flatly, then held out her hand. "Can I have the film please?"

With a finger so light she might have imagined it except she was looking right at him, he scooped back a rogue strand of her hair, tucking it behind her ears. "You look tired," he said softly.

If he only knew. She hadn't slept in days, only snatches here and there. "I can't take the time to rest, not yet."

"You have bruises under your eyes." Bruises he ran his finger over lightly, as if he could remove them with just a touch. "Where have you been sleeping?"

In the back seat of a far too small Honda, bor-rowing the use of a shower when she could, but that sounded pathetic, and her pride reared its ugly head again. "I'll be fine." She continued to hold out her hand for the film. "Just tell me how much."

"No."

"No?" Panic surged. "I need that film, Nick."

He sighed. "Yes, you can have the film. No, you can't pay me. Look, obviously we can't stay here, but I can develop the black-and-white shots at my place. It's here, in Providence. Let me do that for you."

She stared at him, half suspicious, half dying to be able to believe in someone, anyone. "Why?"

"Why?" He looked baffled that she'd even ask. "Do I look like the kind of man who'd let you walk out that door, knowing the trouble you're in? Knowing that your ex could find you at any moment? That the cops are looking for you? That you're scared and alone and probably beyond exhausted, not to mention hungry and broke?"

Her throat burned all the more. "I'm f—"

"Don't say fine. Don't lie, not to me."

"With those pictures, I'll be—"

"Fine," he said in concert with her, and let out a disparaging sound. "Well, your kind of *fine* sucks, Danielle."

"I'm sure you have better plans for the evening than developing the film for me." She didn't know why she pushed him, maybe because hearing him voice his concerns had shaken her. Maybe because she didn't want to be forced to accept help, especially from a man who could melt the walls she'd so carefully built around her heart without even trying.

"At the moment, my only plans are closing up this place so we don't have any more surprise guests." He put the lens cover on the camera. Shut the closet door. Came to stand in front of her; a tall, hauntingly familiar man, looking as if he didn't quite know what to do with her. Reaching out, he took her hand, turned it palm up and dropped the film canister in it. "I can't force you to trust me, or to accept my help—"

"No, you can't."

"But I can ask it of you. Please?"

She tucked the film into her pocket, overwhelmed by both the need to keep running, and the tightness in her chest that indicated she wanted to let him help. "Nick..."

"I know." His voice was low, gruff. "I wouldn't want help, either."

"I'm going to be okay."

"Yeah." He touched her again, just a hand on her arm.

It electrified her.

"But you're running on empty," he said softly, and kept on touching her. "Whether you want to admit it or not, you're going to shut down. Then what?" His finger slid into her hair, his thumb stroking her jaw. "You get Sadie taken away? Maybe put back into the hands of your ex? You get yourself a police record you don't need or deserve?" Lightly, he stroked his hands to her shoulders, which he gently rubbed, right where all the tension had balled into one tight knot.

She nearly melted to the floor.

Then his fingers danced up, slipping beneath her collar now, skin to skin. Her nipples beaded, shocking her. Spontaneous arousal wasn't something she'd experienced in a very long time, and not only did she feel hot and itchy from the inside out, she felt confused. She closed her eyes. "I won't get caught."

"You don't deserve this, Danielle. Come with me." His mouth was close to her ear. Their bodies brushed together. "I can develop the film for you at my place."

"I thought you weren't a photographer."

"Not a professional, no. It's just a hobby, passed down from my father. Come with me."

To his place. "I...couldn't."

"You'd rather sleep in your car again."

Her gaze jerked up to his. "I never said that."

"You didn't have to." He backed away and began shutting off lights, his movements slow and sure, but she had no trouble reading the tension in his tight, tough body.

Every time he passed Sadie, the dog regarded him very seriously, as if still determining whether he could be trusted or not.

Danielle did the same.

Finally, with just the one small light left on in the reception area, he stopped directly in front of her. "Are you going to keep waiting for me to leap out and yell boo?"

She let out a low laugh. "I'm not afraid of you."

But she was, because he threatened the one thing no one else ever had.

Her heart.

# 6

"IF YOU'RE NOT AFRAID, you're nervous," Nick said, seeming annoyed, though not at her. He touched her again, just set one hand on her arm, as if it was natural to keep touching her. "I can understand," he said. "Given what you've been through. But you can stop." He looked into her eyes. "I'm not going to do anything you don't want me to."

She might have laughed, because good Lord, what she suddenly wanted him to do to her! "You keep putting your hands on me."

"So I do," he murmured, still doing exactly that. "Can't seem to help it. Is it bothering you?" As he asked, one hand slid around her waist to rest on the small of her back.

Was it bothering her? It was bothering her pulse, which kept skyrocketing.

"Danielle?" His free hand cupped her jaw.

"No." She lifted her own hand, setting it on his against her face. "But you should know, I'm not interested in—" She broke off because she *was* interested. Too much.

Now his fingers slid over her lips to stop any more lies. He watched her mouth with a heat that made her knees weak. In the depths of his gaze she saw an uncertainty she knew matched her own. He was as unsettled as she with this strange, inexplicable feeling.

Good.

If they were both unsettled, they could leave it alone.

"Come with me," he said. "I'll develop the film. You'll sleep. Catch up. Give yourself at least that much of a head start, okay?"

One night. So tempting. Then she'd be on her way—alone except for Sadie.

As she was meant to be. "One night?"

"One night." With a hand still low on her spine, he leaned in close, reaching past her to flip off the last light. His chest brushed hers. So did his hips.

And all the spots in between sort of melded together. *One night.* It shocked her to her toes what she suddenly wanted to do with their one night.

He was tough and sinewy and warm. Her nipples were still hard and achy, and she didn't quite manage to contain the little sound that escaped her throat, that sounded like the one Sadie made when she wanted to be stroked.

His eyes, dark and full of heat, met Danielle's. "You okay?"

No, actually, she wasn't. Her body was on fire. It felt as if it had been taken over by an alien. An alien whose entire purpose was to obtain as much pleasure as possible.

Not that she didn't enjoy pleasure, but she'd sort of foregone such a thing for other, more important things, like survival. "It's just that...I'm not used to—" Embarrassed, she broke off. "Well. You know."

"Yeah." There was a rough timbre to his tone and a darkness in the depths of his eyes. His fingers flexed on her lower back, then relaxed. Though he spoke utterly calmly, the bulge between his thighs, the one pressing against her lower belly, belied that calmness. "I can't help my reaction to you, Danielle. I mean, look at you. You're beautiful. Smart. Fascinating." When she scoffed and tried to look away, he held her still. "You excite me," he said very quietly. "You always have."

"Really?"

"Really. But I happen to be able to control myself. We're going to my house to develop your film because staying here is a bad idea. And we're going to get you some much-needed rest. Okay?"

She stared at him for a long moment, then nodded. "The film and the rest part. But I don't know about the stay-over part."

"One thing at a time, then."

"Yes," she whispered.

His smile was slow, and somehow both sweet and hot at the same time. Good thing he still had his hands on her, she needed the support. But then he backed away with a wry grimace. "I haven't had this sort of problem since high school."

"Problem?"

Now the wry grimace turned into a wry laugh, and he shoved his fingers through his hair, disturbing it, before cramming his hands deep in his pockets. "Uncontrollable erections."

"Oh," she said, her face flaming, and unable to control it, her gaze was suddenly glued to the spot in question.

"That will make it worse," he said very silkily.

Putting her hands to her hot cheeks, she turned away.

NICK STOOD next to Danielle in the darkened studio knowing he was in trouble. He just wasn't sure how he'd managed to get there.

He was taking her home with him because she needed him.

Okay, not entirely. It was just that he felt loath to let her walk right back out of his life as if nothing had happened.

And nothing *had* happened.

Unless one counted the way his heart had leaped into his throat at just the sight of her. Maybe if he didn't look at her...

He looked at Sadie instead. "She looks hot," he said, watching the huge dog pant.

"She needs water."

"Here, then. Before we go." He backed into the office, opened the darkroom and took out a bin. He was used to the dark in here, unlike Danielle, who bumped into his chest.

"Oh," she said, flattening her palm over his heart.

At the light touch, his blood pounded. He'd dreamed about her during his most impressionable adolescent years, but this was ridiculous. "Wait right here." Moving away from her, he filled the bin from the cold water in the sink, then set it down for Sadie.

The dog pressed between them, diving for the water. No dainty lapping for this dog. She stuck her entire face in and slurped at it, making water splash over the sides onto the floor, his shoes, everywhere.

Then she lifted her head, looked right into his eyes and let out a sharp bark, nearly piercing his eardrums.

"She's thanking you."

He studied the dog, who had water all over her face, running in two long streams out either side of her mouth. He thought about the mess on the floor and what his sisters would say. Thought about how he was going to have to get down on his hands and knees and scrub. He sighed. "She's welcome." He'd come back tomorrow and clean up. When his life returned to normal and he was back on vacation, with nothing demanding his time or efforts.

Just then Danielle's scent came to him—clean woman—and he found himself inhaling deeply, wanting to bury his face in her hair. "Let's go," he said a little gruffly.

They were on the steps outside when he heard the car pull up. Beside him, Danielle tensed, and so did Sadie.

Nick looked into the street and got a little tense himself. Damn it, he'd forgotten something that had seemed so important to him only a few hours before.

His date with...ah, hell. Muffy? Missy? He couldn't quite remember her name. They'd met in a bar only two nights ago and the place had been incredibly noisy.

By arrangement, they were to meet here at six o'clock. It couldn't be that late already, could it? But one glance at his watch assured him it could and was.

"Yoo-hoo!" His date waved from her car as she double-parked. Then Missy...Muffy... No, Molly. *Molly* leapt out the driver's door, her wild blond hair cascading down her back in ringlets, her short, short, short gold sundress shimmering in the sun. Mile-long legs strutted. Full, round breasts jiggled as she hurried toward him, smiling with that wide, painted mouth he'd thought so sexy only a few nights before.

Now, though it felt cruel to think it, she seemed like nothing more than a toy, and he couldn't imagine what he'd been thinking to ask her out. Maybe thinking hadn't been involved. After all, they had nothing in common, nothing to talk about. She was nothing like...

Danielle.

"Hey there," Molly purred, reaching them. She glanced at Danielle curiously but without any animosity, probably figuring Danielle far too plain, too quiet, too reserved for Nick's taste.

She couldn't have been more wrong. To Nick, Danielle's soft expression, her beautiful and not made-up eyes, her tasteful clothes, was a package proving to be more desirable than he could have imagined. "Molly." He stepped closer, trying to head her off. "I'm sorry," he started regretfully, reaching out for her hand in order to avoid—

Nope, no avoiding it. Molly drew him in, squeezing him in a hug that smothered him in perfume and undoubtedly left lipstick where she'd planted her red mouth to the side of his.

Over her shoulder, he caught a glimpse of Danielle, who was doing a great impression of someone who could care less, but in her eyes was a hurt that tugged at something deep inside of him.

"Wait until you see what I've got on beneath this dress," Molly whispered in his ear.

Feeling stupid and awkward, he pulled back. "I'm sorry," he said again, looking into her eyes, watching as they filled with disappointment. "But—"

"You're canceling." Molly sighed. "Is it the

hairdo?" She patted the over-the-top curls. "Too wild, huh? Or maybe the nails—" She held out metallic blue nails imprinted with little white letters that spelled erogenous zones of the human anatomy.

"It has nothing to do with how you look. You look..." Ah, hell. He was no good at this. "Molly, it's just that an old friend stopped by, and she needs some help, and—"

"Oh, I understand." Molly eyed the silent Danielle again, then smiled. "We'll reschedule, then?"

He looked into her hopeful expression, crossed his fingers and nodded. "Another time."

"'Kay." Leaning forward, giving him an ample view of her generous breasts, she kissed him one last time. "See you soon," she whispered with promise in her sultry voice. "Ta!"

Nick waited until Molly had gotten into her car and driven off before turning to Danielle. "Uh...do you want to follow me? Or drive in my car and we'll come back for yours later?"

Her smile was brittle, her voice downright chilly. "Definitely, I'll follow." She pulled out a set of keys and didn't look at him. "Didn't mean to mess up your plans for the evening—"

"Danielle, I'm sorry. I'd forgotten—"

She turned to him. "Look, let's get this over with, okay? The sooner the better, and then you can catch up with your...girlfriend." She tried to go around him but he blocked her.

"She's not my girlfriend."

"Whatever."

She stopped trying to get around him and glared into his face. "That shade of lipstick really doesn't become you." Then she sashayed past him, her slim hips and curvy little butt wriggling with attitude and bad temper.

TED BLACKSTONE couldn't believe it. She'd left him. Danielle Douglass, the woman he'd thought so perfect for him, a complement to the rest of his life, had up and walked out.

No one had ever walked out on him.

He'd grown up with the power of influential parents, and while he'd never actually spent much time in their company—they'd been too busy making money—he'd always enjoyed the fruits of their success.

Later, as a formidable investor in his own right, he'd had the world at his own fingertips. Fabulous house, great car, nice bank account...but still, as always, he'd been...lonely.

Until Danielle.

She'd looked at him with worship. He was her world, and God, he'd loved it...and her. After he'd neatly folded her life into his, he'd finally felt satisfied. At peace. He'd had it all, even a champion show dog for added pride and glory.

He loved glory.

Oh yeah, things had been good. But then he'd made a few bad judgements on the market. He'd been forced to dip into his trust fund, and then, out of desperation, had kept dipping. In the blink of an eye his fat bank account had gone on an alarming diet, and his car and house were in jeopardy.

To top off the indignity of it all, Danielle, his beloved Danielle, had left him, stealing his prized show dog—the only investment he had left that was worth anything—in the process. He wanted it all back.

Especially Danielle. And what Ted Blackstone wanted, he always got.

# 7

DANIELLE FOLLOWED Nick in her borrowed car, doubting herself the entire way there. In fact, she didn't even know where *there* was, other than they weren't leaving Providence. She knew almost nothing about the man she'd somehow ended up trusting. Again.

Nick Cooper. It was still hard to believe. He'd been the most interesting person in her high school, not because of status, or jockhood, or that he kissed like absolute heaven. Which he did.

But because he hadn't cared what others thought of him. It was a rare person who had that much confidence, and that he'd had it so young had really struck a chord with her.

He still had it in spades.

And he had something else that never failed to amaze her.

Kindness.

"Doesn't say much for me," she muttered. "That

a sweet word and a light touch leaves me following after him like a dog."

Sadie shot her a baleful glance out of her dark eyes.

"Sorry." Danielle stroked the dog's massive head. "It wasn't just the kindness anyway." She sighed and downshifted as she followed him into a town house complex that was very classy, very New England. "You **might** have noticed how remarkable-looking he is."

Sadie yawned.

"Right." They were on a secluded side street, lined with oak trees and wildflowers and groomed lawns. There were no fenced yards in sight, which probably meant dogs weren't welcome.

Nick parked, and she stopped next to him, but didn't get out of the car, not yet.

He came around and leaned on his passenger door, long legs crossed, hands in his pockets. Lazily, he thrust his chin toward the lovely two-story town house in front of them. "That's mine."

"It's...nice."

He shook his head and laughed. "You should know, you have a caged-in look about you." Casual as you pleased, he smiled. "So why don't you tell me what you think is going to happen up there?"

"Absolutely nothing." She bit her lower lip. "Right?"

Pushing away from the door, his smile still in place, though now his eyes held a grimness she didn't understand, he opened her door.

She expected him to pull her from the car. Maybe sidetrack her with another smile and a touch of his warm, strong hands.

She didn't expect him to hunker down at her side, right at eye level and just look at her.

Staring in front of her out the windshield, she ignored him.

But unlike Ted, who'd always seemed to have a lot to say, Nick said nothing.

She fiddled with her seat belt. Touched her backpack. Chewed her lip. *"What?"* she finally demanded, her gaze whipping back to his. "What are you looking at?"

"You tell me."

"I don't want to play any guessing games here, Nick."

"Funny. Me, either." He set a hand on hers, over the steering wheel. "Come up. Get your pictures. Get some rest. The end. Can you do that?"

"Especially the end part."

Now his smile reached his eyes. "That's a girl. One step at a time, right? Let's go."

One step at a time. Easier than it sounded, but she got out of the car and grabbed Sadie's leash. She hadn't wanted to put him out, hadn't wanted to be any sort of burden, but she'd already blown his obvious plans for the evening with the human Barbie Doll.

And as it had been all those years before, he hadn't said a word to make her feel bad, not one. Hadn't told her how stupid she'd been to get into this ridiculous situation in the first place.

Hard as it was to accept the help, after so many nights in the cramped car if he had so much as a comfortable chair for her to nap in, she'd be eternally grateful.

He led her through the small front yard. On either side, there were impeccable gardens. Grass so green and thick one could get lost in it, flowers of every hue in the rainbow.

In contrast, Nick's yard was mostly brick, with two large potted trees.

"Low maintenance," he said, putting his key in the lock. "I'm gone for long stretches. No need to keep killing pretty flowers with my neglect." He gestured her in first.

But Danielle hesitated. "What about Sadie?"

"Does she have an aversion to being inside?"

"No."

"Well, then, show her in."

"She's..." Danielle looked down at Sadie, knowing that while the dog was her own personal treasure, she was also not easy. "She can be a bit messy."

"I hadn't noticed," he said dryly, waiting with that same calm patience he'd shown her since she'd first walked into the photo studio. The same calm patience he'd shown her all those years ago.

"Be good," she whispered to the dog.

"Make yourself at home." Nick took them through a wide, open living room sparsely furnished with light oak furniture, photographs from all over the world and the biggest couch she'd ever seen.

Covered in cushions, it was dark forest green and so inviting she nearly crumpled on it right then and there. Her body actually leaned toward it, begging, but Nick kept walking.

With an exhausted sigh, she followed, Sadie in tow, her toenails clicking on the hardwood floors.

The kitchen was light and airy, too. There was a basket of fruit on the counter that had her mouth watering. And a loaf of bread right next to it.

When had she last eaten? There'd been the burger for lunch, but nothing for breakfast...

Nick opened the refrigerator. "You're in luck, I actually bought some food the other day. Usually this place is empty. What would you like?"

"The photos."

"Yes, your pictures," he said with the first hint of impatience in his voice. "But first, food. When did you last eat? *What* did you last eat?" He craned his neck and looked her over. "You look like a good wind could blow you over. Never mind," he said in disgust when she just lifted her chin. "Good God, why would anyone ask a woman what she wants to eat? She'll say nothing, and then just as likely eat everything on my plate. We'll have soup and sandwiches," he decided, talking to himself now. "Fast and filling."

Pride warred with fierce hunger at the thought of hot soup and a big sandwich. "Do you always feed perfect strangers just because they look hungry?"

"We're hardly perfect," he said calmly, opening a can of soup, pouring it into a pot and putting it on the stove. Then he pulled out the sandwich fixings and started working, as if he were an old pro in the kitchen.

She tried not to notice how utterly sexy he looked concentrating at putting mustard on bread.

"And as for the strangers part..." He lifted his head and pierced her with a hot, intimate look that curled her toes. "I already told you. I stopped thinking of you as a stranger long ago."

She forced her gaze back to the job at hand—food. His long, tanned fingers delicately placed lettuce on the bread. "High school was a long time ago."

He nodded, his mouth curving in memories.

Helpless to resist the lure of the thick turkey he was now layering over the lettuce, she moved closer. "You...haven't forgotten how horrible it was."

"I've forgotten nothing."

"I've never really forgiven myself for those days."

"You sure enjoy paying for the sins of others, don't you?" He leveled his timber-green eyes on hers while he brought his hand up and sucked a drop of mustard off his thumb. "It wasn't your crowd I dreamed about."

"Oh."

"Yeah." A smile grew. "*Oh.*"

She looked into his now-mischievous gaze, her heart catching at what she saw in it. "You really dreamed..."

"Oh baby, you have no idea how many fantasies you headlined for me over those years."

She actually looked behind her. "*Me?*"

"You."

"Well, that's..." Thrilling. Tantalizing. *Terrifying.* "Disgusting."

Still smiling, he looked unconcerned. "Most high school boys are. And I was all boy." He went back to the sandwiches, adding cheese.

"You really had...sexual dreams about me?"

"Hmm." He sucked his thumb again, closing his eyes, a fully sensual, passionate creature, enjoying every possible sensation. "Good dreams, too," he murmured, his voice impossibly husky. "Did I mention I had a great imagination?" His gaze, scalding now, skimmed over her from head to toe, then slowly back again. "And even in my wildest dreams, I never, ever, put you together as good as the reality."

He poured her a bowl of soup from the stove, loaded one sandwich on a plate, then dumped half a bag of potato chips on it. "Enjoy," he said lightly, gently shoving her onto a bar stool at the counter.

He turned back to the cutting board and chopped up some turkey and cheese. Then he set it into a bowl and eyed Sadie. "Watch my fingers, dog," he warned, putting it on the floor.

Sadie charged at the bowl, and Nick nearly fell over backward, trying to get out of the way.

Danielle would have laughed, except...he'd fed her dog. Unprompted. Just...fed her.

"Holy smokes," he said, still staring at Sadie.

Sounds of Sadie's chomping filled the air. Her tail beat the air as she swallowed everything in the bowl in two seconds flat.

"She likes her food," she whispered through a clogged throat.

"She was starving," he said, sounding horrified.

"No, she always eats like that."

He continued to stare at her, carefully staying out of tail-wagging range, clearly realizing that it was a tail that could slice a man in two. "Wow."

Danielle lifted her sandwich to her mouth, then nearly moaned at her first bite. She swallowed hard when he watched her, because there was just something about the way she received his entire, undivided attention that both unnerved and aroused her at the same time. "Nick..."

"Yeah?"

"Thank you."

He broke eye contact to get his own sandwich, and she took a good second look at him. And a third. Not because he was so beautiful he stole her breath—which he did—and not because she wanted him in a way that made her ache—though that was true, too—but because there was something...

Being thanked made him uncomfortable.

Having wolfed down his sandwich, he held up the film canister. "I'm going to go get this started."

"Yes, but—"

"I converted the third bathroom into a darkroom eons ago. I'll just be down the hall if you need me."

"Nick—"

"Hold that thought."

He didn't want to be thanked. Well, fine. But then he needed to stop putting her in his debt. That wouldn't happen until she left.

She'd go back to being alone. Back to her bone-weariness and fear. She'd go, and as quickly as she could.

She'd go, mostly because an inexplicable part of her didn't want to.

WHEN NICK EMERGED from the darkroom, everything was silent. Far too silent for having a monster of a dog in the house. Curious, he walked through the living room to the kitchen.

Empty.

And clean, he noticed. She'd put everything away, including the bowl Sadie had used.

His deck was empty, too, and his heart picked up speed as he went back into the living room. If she'd left—

Stopping in front of the couch that he hadn't even glanced at before, he let out a rough sigh, then squatted down to peer into Danielle's face.

Her eyes were closed, of course, her lashes long and dark against her skin that was so pale it was nearly translucent. Her hair tumbled over shoulders that looked too thin and vulnerable to be carrying such troubles. In her sleep, she let out a soft sigh, a whimper really.

"Shh," he whispered, and at the sound of his voice, she relaxed.

And just like that, his heart took a tumble. Almost on their own, his fingers lifted to scoop her hair from her face.

A low growl stopped him.

"Yeah, yeah," he murmured, not even glancing at the dog who lay at his feet. "I know. She's yours."

"I'm no one's." Danielle's eyes opened, though not another inch of her moved. "I wasn't sleeping," she said defensively.

"Of course not," he said easily, still sitting on his haunches, his face only inches from hers. "Because that would be resting your body, which, by the way, needs it desperately."

"Did you develop the film?"

"If I say yes, are you leaving?"

"I need to."

"Uh-huh."

She sat up and pushed her hair from her face. "That was a loaded 'uh-huh.'"

"Was it?"

"With a 'you're not rested' in it. With a 'you need a plan' and an 'I don't think you're being smart about this whole thing' added in."

He smiled, even though when she shifted, their knees brushed together. He could imagine her legs smooth and silky against his rougher ones. "You sure heard a lot in that one uh-huh." He put his hand over hers. "Stay tonight, Danielle. Sleep in my bed. *Alone*—" he added when her eyes narrowed. "Get the sleep you need, get some more food in your system and your brain will be so much clearer for it."

"What about your date?"

"You heard me cancel it."

"Yes. I'm...sorry about that."

"Funny." He studied her even features. "You don't look sorry. You look tired, and maybe a little out of sorts—"

"Gee, thanks—"

"But not sorry, not in the least."

"Well, I wasn't jealous or anything." Her cute little nose thrust in the air high enough to give her a nosebleed. "Your time is certainly your own."

"Certainly." He bit back his grin and reached out, stroking a thumb over her arm, playing with the material of her shirt at the shoulder, then under, touching even more skin. Oh yeah, he liked her skin, and the way her breath hitched. He liked that very much.

"You could be having much more fun right this minute," she said a little shakily. "I bet she...would have...*well*."

"Maybe I didn't want to...*well*," he said, mocking her. "Not with her."

"Any man with blood in his body would have wanted to."

"Not me. Stay, Danielle."

Her eyes locked on his, wide and searching. "I'll still have to get out of town in the morning."

"Yes." He surged to his feet, pulling her up with him. She staggered a bit, and because he was a male, and a weak one at that, his hands nudged her and she fell against him.

He held her close, and amazingly enough, she let him, even leaned on him, just for a moment.

Then she pulled free, ran a self-conscious hand down her hair and avoided his gaze.

"Here." He took her down the hall and showed her the bathroom. "Take a shower if you'd like." She looked so grateful and anxious to do just that, it hurt to even look at her. "Then..." He opened his bedroom door, wincing slightly because he hadn't made his bed or cleaned up his clothes from yesterday, which were scattered across the floor. Kicking as many as he could beneath the bed, he jerked up the sheet and blanket, and caught her smiling. "What?"

"You really weren't going to bring your date back here."

"Of course not," he said. Muffy—Molly, damn

it, *Molly* had offered her place. Not that it would have mattered. He'd never felt the need to change anything about himself or his house for others.

Though it didn't escape him that if he'd known Danielle was going to be sleeping in his room, he definitely would have cleaned it.

Danielle laughed and, feeling a little left out as that laughter was clearly aimed at him, he put his hands on his hips and cocked a brow. "What's so funny now?"

"It's just that I pictured the two of you..."

"Pictured us...?"

Her face went a little pink. "She's so pretty, you know, and wearing that dress, I thought you'd—"

"Drag her back here and ravish her?"

"Yes." She shrugged and didn't meet his gaze. "Yes. Exactly."

She'd pictured that? It must have been quite explicit, given the color on her cheeks. Still, Nick had to admit, there might have been plenty of ravishing going on, if Danielle hadn't come along.

But she had, and now he couldn't even imagine being with Molly tonight, which disturbed him.

"Here." From his drawer, he pulled a pair of sweats and a T-shirt. "If you need fresh clothes to sleep in."

She hugged the clothes to her chest and stared at him with those gray eyes that fifteen years ago he would have happily drowned in.

But he was older now. Wiser. She shouldn't have still gotten to him.

And yet she did, in a big way. "Good night," he said gruffly, pushing past her.

But when he got to the door, she called his name.

Not wanting to look back, badly needing to escape, he put his hand on the wood and reluctantly stopped. Slowly he turned, catching her dark gaze. "Yeah?"

"I don't want to take your bed. Please, Nick, the couch is more than fine."

She had the same look on her face that she'd had at her prom. Surprise that he cared. Had so few people cared? It made his throat ache. "Take the bed."

"Nick—"

"Take the bed," he repeated, and shut the door.

Then he did as he did whenever he needed to clear his head; he went for a long, punishing run.

# 8

WHEN NICK GOT BACK, the house was quiet. His bedroom door was shut, and as there was no sign of the dog, he assumed Danielle had her, and that they were both asleep.

Good. He was hot and sweaty and pleasantly exhausted from his run. If he could grab a shower and fall asleep without kicking his brain into high drive, things would be even better.

He managed the shower part of the plan, and settled facedown on the couch. He made himself as comfortable as he could and closed his eyes.

Then, as if on cue, his thoughts started racing.

Danielle was in his bed. In his clothes. Was she curled into a little ball beneath his covers? Or was she sprawled out, taking up the entire bed?

He supposed as long as Sadie was on the floor, it didn't matter, but he couldn't dispel the images of Danielle in his sheets. Bare legs, maybe a creamy shoulder peeking out of his T-shirt. No bra, so her breasts would swing free with her every movement, the nipples hard and pouty, pressing against the material.

Oh yeah, that image would help him sleep. With a rough sigh, he flipped over and studied the ceiling. This was going to be one hell of a long night.

"Nick?" The woman of his dreams materialized at his side. "I couldn't sleep," she whispered, then knelt by his shoulder.

As he'd already discovered, the reality of her was far more potent than any fantasy. She indeed wore his sweats, but because they were big, the waist sagged low on her hips. She'd tied the T-shirt in a knot above her belly button, so there was a gap between the shirt and pants, leaving a good four inches of bare, silky skin.

Right in front of his waiting mouth.

"I wanted to thank you again," she whispered.

He forced his gaze up, up, up, past that bare, tantalizing belly, past the curved globes of her breasts, past her slender throat to her eyes. "Thank me?"

"Because of you, I can let my guard down, if only for tonight."

*No. Bad idea. Don't let your guard down.*

"You took me in without mentioning how foolish I am to get myself into this situation."

"I don't think you're foolish."

"Thank you for that, too," she said very softly. "You gave me food and shelter, and—" Her voice cracked. Her eyes misty, she gave him a watery smile.

Ah, hell.

"Nick..."

He wanted to tell her not to say his name that way, that quiet, warm way that stabbed through all his protective layers. He had lots of those layers, had built them for a young, rather geeky kid, then more for his worldly travels to prevent what he saw and reported on from touching him too much. Layers so that no one person had ever had a grip on his heart.

"I'll leave in the morning," she said softly, in that voice that reminded him they did have a past, no matter how tenuous it was. "But I want what we should have had all those years ago. I want this night, with you. Make love to me, Nick. Please?"

DANIELLE WAITED with bated breath for his answer. Ted had always hated it when she'd made the first move, but she was making it now.

Did she have it right?

Lying in bed, alone, worrying, obsessing, had done her no good. The only thing that had worked was thinking about Nick. He'd been there for her in a way no one else ever had, and she wanted to give him something in return.

But wanting him to make love to her wasn't all altruistic. No way, not when her breath stuttered whenever she so much as looked at him. She wanted to give him more than her gratitude, she wanted to get a taste of what she should have allowed herself all those years ago. She wanted to be held in those strong hard arms, wanted to lose herself in quick, selfish, mind-blowing passion.

And then, when it was over, when night turned to dawn, she'd get up and walk away, holding those memories tight forever.

"Please?" she whispered, tugging at the light blanket he'd thrown over himself.

Beneath it, Lord, beneath it his body was beautiful; long and muscular, showing the strength of a man who used it and often. To her regret, he wasn't completely naked. He wore a pair of dark gray knit boxers, which snugly clung to his muscled thighs and...other interesting parts.

She couldn't tear her eyes away.

"Danielle."

She looked into his eyes as he touched her jaw, startled by all she saw there, so much so that she closed her own eyes, turning her face into his light touch.

But she wanted more, so much more. He could give her that something more. He represented warmth and strength and an end to being alone, if only for tonight. So she ran her fingers along the light stubble on his hard jawline, over the mouth she wanted to feel on hers. "Nick...love me."

"You're confusing comfort with sex," he said in a rough whisper. "Take it from someone who's done the same often enough to know. I can't let you—"

"Nick." She watched his eyes darken at the sound of his name on her lips, and she whispered it again. And then again, when his hand drifted down her neck onto her shoulder, then glided lightly over her arm down to her fingers, which he entwined with his.

Something shivered through her at the sweet, romantic gesture, and she told herself it was desire, not something more. Not any sort of emotional connection.

"It should be more," he said, reading her mind.

Maybe, but it couldn't be. This and only this was within her reach. One mindless night, with him.

Feeling bold, she sat back on her heels and pulled the T-shirt over her head and off.

His breath caught. His mouth fell open, then shut with an audible snap. "Danielle," he said hoarsely.

Never in her life had she been so shameless, but also something else. Wicked and brazen, and...free. *Free*, for the first time in too long.

Coming to her feet, she tugged on the tie of the sweats he'd given her. Then gave them a little push as she wriggled her hips, letting the material slowly slip down her thighs, leaving her only in a pair of panties.

His eyes glued to her body, he sucked in a breath and swallowed hard. "Danielle."

"Please don't turn me away." She sat at his hip, her heart in her throat because she needed this, needed him, more than she needed her next breath.

He let out a groan and reached for her, tugging her down over the top of him, drawing her closer to his oh-so-warm body. His breath skimmed her temple, her hair, while his hands molded and possessed her, stoking the ache deep within her to blind, primitive need.

He seemed to be similarly affected. Scooping her hair back from her face in fistfuls, he drew her close, staring into her eyes until their lips touched in a long, melting kiss. Then he let her hair go to trail those talented, greedy hands down her sides, stroking her breasts, holding her up so that he could look at her nipples, which were thrust near his face, begging for attention. He put his mouth on one, drawing it into his mouth, using his tongue and teeth, until she cried out, hips arching into his. Pulling back enough to blow a hot breath on the wet nipple, he slid his hands over her, down her back, and then lower, cupping two handfuls of her bottom.

Her pulse had long ago scrambled, and now so did her senses. They had all night, she thought with a bittersweet mixture of joy and misery. She could make the most of every hour, every single second. Knowing that, she pressed into him, eliciting a rough growl.

"Is this what you had in mind?" he asked a bit roughly, slipping his hands into her panties, his fingers dipping and exploring.

She let out a helpless little moan.

"Is it?"

"Yes," she gasped, as his hands slid between her thighs to where she was already creamy, hot and very, very wet. "Yes," she gasped again when he hooked his thumbs in her panties, and holding her gaze prisoner in his own, slowly worked them down.

"Better." He tossed them into the air, returning his hands to her body with a low groan. "Much better, but—"

A low whine jerked her right out of her sensual haze, as they both turned their heads. Nick let out a groaning laugh.

Sadie sat at their side, a pair of panties draped over one bloodshot eye, head cocked as she studied them closely. "Woof," she offered, close enough to blast them with doggie breath.

Danielle's muscles, tight and trembling under Nick's incredible touch only seconds ago, let go, and she sagged over him. "Go to sleep, Sadie." *Please.*

Sadie sat up straighter, still panting.

"Lay down," Danielle pleaded. "Go on now."

More panting.

Danielle looked into Nick's frustrated but laughing eyes. "She failed obedience."

"I'm shocked." Nick narrowed his eyes and studied Sadie. "Is it my imagination, or is she getting ready to bite something?"

Sadie's big tongue swiped over her mouth in a

way that did indeed make her appear to be licking her chops in preparation of chowing down on something.

Or someone.

"Don't worry, she hardly ever bites."

"Oh, good."

"We could just pretend she isn't here," Danielle suggested hopefully, noticing how nice Nick's bare chest felt brushing her equally bare nipples.

Nick noticed how nice it felt, too, evidenced by the impressive bulge currently pressing insistently against her thigh.

"Just ignore her," she tried desperately, slipping down for a kiss. He was such a good kisser, so warm and generous and...still staring at Sadie.

Who was staring right back at him.

Danielle covered Nick's eyes and tried to deepen the kiss but it was no good. She most definitely did not have his entire attention. With a sigh, she sat up on him.

"Call me a prude," he said. "But I've never actually had an audience before. It's a bit unnerving."

"Yeah." Feeling very naked, she stood and reached for the panties still hanging off Sadie's ear and the T-shirt on the floor.

Before she could put them on, Nick came to his feet and pressed up behind her, slipping his arms around her waist. His forearms were tanned, tough and strewn with sinew against her fair-skinned, soft stomach, and when he slipped his hands up to cup her breasts, she nearly cried.

"Is she still watching me?" he murmured in her ear, his fingers stroking her nipples.

She wanted to melt, but managed to crane her neck toward Sadie.

Who had her gaze glued to a spot Danielle wanted to stare at as well.

Nick's butt.

"I'm trying not to notice," he said. His arms squeezed her close. "You feel so good against me, Danielle. So good. But—"

"No. No buts." Her body was so keyed up, she couldn't walk away now. Words were beyond her so she turned and showed him what she wanted with her body, sliding against him, gliding her breasts over his chest, her hips to the spot between his where he was hard and heavy.

"Foul," he whispered, and with a movement that left her gasping in surprise, he scooped her into his arms and started down the hall.

"Hurry," she whispered, then arched her naked body in his arms.

With a groan, he stopped in the middle of the hallway, pressing her against the wall, holding her there with his delicious body. His mouth took hers, and then, breathless, he lifted his head. "You're sure you want this?"

"More than air."

With a smile that tipped her heart on its side, he indulged them both in another long, lingering kiss. Finally, finally, he carried her into his bedroom and kicked the door closed behind them. Lifting his head, he asked, "Can she open doors?"

Danielle couldn't think past the sight of the bed that she hoped he intended to ravish her on. "Who?"

"The man-eater."

Oh Lord, the way he was eating her up with his gaze. "No, Sadie can't open doors."

"Good." With his mouth teasing her jaw, he set her on the bed, his hands never leaving her body. A soft touch here, there...over her breasts, her nipples, her belly...between her thighs, urging her legs open so that he could watch while he stroked her to a slow burn with an erotic touch such as she'd never known before.

She was quivering now, with each stroke, helplessly arching into him. "Nick..."

"Yeah." His fingers sank into her wet heat, and he let out a rough groan from deep in his throat.

"Now," she heard herself cry, thrusting her hips against him. "Oh, please now..." She reached for him, but he evaded, gently but thoroughly capturing her hands, then pressing her back, his body covering hers. "If you touch me now, it'll be over before it begins."

"Then we'll start again!"

Nick liked the sound of that, starting again. Her voice sounded thready, desperate, and her long legs wrapped around his hips so that he nearly sank into her. As he was feeling thready and desperate himself, it took every ounce of control he had to hold back.

Sliding down her body, he used his mouth everywhere he passed. Her nipples, her belly, high on her thigh, close to the one spot that would drive her over the edge, close, but not close enough.

"Nick!" Her eyes clouded over, her hands still at her sides, held by his, flexed.

"I know." He released her to slide his hands over her thighs, opening them even farther, to lick her, *there*.

With a screech, she arched up off the bed, right into his mouth. "Perfect," he whispered, and slowly and thoroughly devoured her.

She tried to hold back from him. Clearly, this was not the hot and fast she'd intended, but he refused to give that to her. This was no quick fix, this was more. And if he had to know it, recognize it, then so did she. "Come for me," he whispered against her.

And she did, with a wild abandon that thrilled and aroused him all the more.

Damp flesh slid over damp flesh as he slid back up her body, every bit as hostage to this vicious need as she. He rubbed his cheek to hers as she fluttered her eyes open. "There's still more," he said.

"Yes." She tried to draw him inside her body. "For you."

"For both of us." Putting on a condom was tricky, as his hands were shaking. *Shaking.* Danielle didn't help matters by lending her ineffective yet overwhelmingly arousing fingers to the task. Finally, he lifted her hips, stared deep into her eyes and sank into her.

She took him, every inch, then let him in even deeper.

"This," he managed to say, fighting back the tide that threatened to take him over the edge with his first stroke. "This is more. For both of us." And lowering his mouth to hers, he began to move.

# 9

NICK AWOKE IN THE DARK. From what he could gather with his few still-functioning senses, he was sprawled on his back, sideways across the bed. Given the breeze blowing across his lower parts he concluded the window was open. As for the restriction of air to his lungs, that was Danielle, who lay a deadweight on his chest.

She was also buck naked, which happened to agree with him.

Grinning, he slid her off, then settled himself between her legs. Murmuring something sleepily, she slipped her arms around him. "Nick?"

God, that voice. It did things to his insides, things he wasn't ready to face, so he concentrated on what she did to him physically.

And physically, he wanted her again. "Yeah, it's me. You're so beautiful, Danielle."

"It's dark."

"It doesn't matter."

"Oh, Nick."

"Open for me."

Arching up, she wrapped her legs around his hips.

"Yeah, like that." Tilting her face up for his kiss, he sank into her body and took her again. Took them both to a place he'd never been with anyone ever before.

THE NEXT TIME Nick woke up, morning light slanted in through the windows, making him squint as he reached out for...nobody.

Given that the pillow he'd shared with Danielle all night long felt cold, he sat straight up, his heart in his throat.

And came face to face with a monster, a huge monster with dark, red-rimmed eyes and incisors capable of gobbling him up in one bite.

With a shocked gasp, he jerked back.

The monster leapt back, too, and let out a sharp, surprised bark.

"Damn it." Flat on his back in the middle of the bed, Nick blinked at the ceiling and tried to recover his pulse. "You're giving me gray hair."

The bed shifted as two heavy paws hit it.

Nick craned his neck to the side, eyeing Sadie cautiously. "I suppose you think that's funny."

Head cocked, a line of drool puddling on his sheets, the dog eyed him and licked her chops.

Hastily, Nick scrambled for the sheet. "Don't get any ideas. I'm not edible."

"I wouldn't say that."

Nick lifted his head as Danielle came back into the room. She was dressed in another pair of khaki shorts and a sleeveless blouse—red this time—looking sleek, beautiful and more than a little wary. Her backpack was on her shoulder, her laptop tucked under her arm. She was holding the developed photos he'd given her.

Not a good sign on his chances of coaxing her back into bed.

"I wanted to thank you again," she said quietly, staying by the door.

Uh-oh. Definitely, he had some fast talking to do in order to get lucky. "You're dressed." Oh, *smooth.*

"I've got to go."

*Stall.* Not because he couldn't let her go. Hell, he could let anyone go. He wasn't the attachment sort of guy, but...

Damn it, he couldn't let her go. "Hold on." Eyeing Sadie, he got out of the bed and carefully walked around the dog, feeling very naked. He grabbed a pair of jeans. "At least let me get you some breakfast."

She shifted, trying not to stare around the held-up jeans, but she couldn't seem to help herself, which did stroke his ego somewhat.

And of course, encouraged his morning hard-on. "Nick..."

There was that voice again, the soft, breathy tone that made getting his jeans on nearly a detriment to his health.

Her gaze was glued to his hands as he attempted to get the buttons closed, and when he had to carefully tuck himself inside the denim, she made a sort of choked noise.

"I told you I would have to leave in the morning," she said quickly, when he looked at her.

"Yeah, but that was before last night." Before they'd made love. Now that they had, he'd figured she wouldn't really be able to walk away.

Or maybe *he* was the only one feeling that way.

No. There was heat and desire in her gaze as it lingered over his body, but there was more, too. Angst and a reluctant affection. Very reluctant.

*Ditto, sweetheart, and I'm no more thrilled than you.* Then he pictured her walking out his front door, which made his stomach hurt. "What's the rush?"

# The Harlequin Reader Service® — Here's how it works:

Accepting your 2 free books and gift places you under no obligation to buy anything. You may keep the books and gift and return the shipping statement marked "cancel." If you do not cancel, about a month later we'll send you 4 additional books and bill you just $3.57 each in the U.S., or $4.20 each in Canada, plus 25¢ shipping & handling per book and applicable taxes if any.* That's the complete price and — compared to cover prices of $4.25 each in the U.S. and $4.99 each in Canada — it's quite a bargain! You may cancel at any time, but if you choose to continue, every month we'll send you 4 more books, which you may either purchase at the discount price or return to us and cancel your subscription.

*Terms and prices subject to change without notice. Sales tax applicable in N.Y. Canadian residents will be charged applicable provincial taxes and GST.

If offer card is missing write to: The Harlequin Reader Service, 3010 Walden Ave., P.O. Box 1867, Buffalo, NY 14240-1867

NO POSTAGE
NECESSARY
IF MAILED
IN THE
UNITED STATES

## BUSINESS REPLY MAIL
FIRST-CLASS MAIL    PERMIT NO. 717-003    BUFFALO, NY

POSTAGE WILL BE PAID BY ADDRESSEE

HARLEQUIN READER SERVICE
3010 WALDEN AVE
PO BOX 1867
BUFFALO NY 14240-9952

**Do You Have the LUCKY KEY?**

# PLAY THE *Lucky Key Game*

*and you can get*

# FREE BOOKS and a FREE GIFT!

Scratch the gold areas with a coin. Then check below to see the books and gift you can get!

**YES!** I have scratched off the gold areas. Please send me the 2 FREE BOOKS and GIFT for which I qualify. I understand I am under no obligation to purchase any books, as explained on the back of this card.

342 HDL DNV3                     142 HDL DNVR

| | |
|---|---|
| FIRST NAME | LAST NAME |

ADDRESS

APT.#          CITY

STATE/PROV.          ZIP/POSTAL CODE

🔑🔑🔑🔑 2 free books plus a free gift          🔑🔑🔑🔑 1 free book

🔑🔑🔑🔑 2 free books          🔑🔑🔑🔑 Try Again!

Offer limited to one per household and not valid to current
Harlequin Temptation® subscribers. All orders subject to approval.

*Visit us online at*
**www.eHarlequin.com**

"You know what my rush is."

"Just breakfast, Danielle. Not a marriage proposal."

She flushed. "I don't need either. I've called Emma. She's the friend I borrowed the car from, and she needs it back today. She's getting a ride over here, then she'll take me to Donald, the art director I told you about."

"Where you'll show him Sadie's pictures, he'll pay you enough to buy another car and you'll jump town to start a new life. Happily ever after, right?" He shook his head. "Tell me you're not that gullible."

"It could happen."

"Yeah, but there's sure a lot of things that could go wrong." He stalked to his closet, hauled out a shirt and jammed his arms into it. "Too many things."

A honk sounded outside from the street.

Danielle froze, stared at Nick. "There she is."

When she turned to go, he grabbed her arm. "Wait."

"I can't, I—"

"Yeah, I know. You've got to go. But how well do you know this Emma? And Donald? Are they friends of yours? Good friends?"

"Well, of course." But she didn't look him in the eyes. "I know them because of the industry, of course, but—" Another honk sounded and she looked up at him entreatingly. "Please. Don't make this harder than it already is."

"Industry friends." He followed her down the hall, eyes glued to the gentle sway of her hips. He'd be happy following her like a damn puppy dog every single morning.

She opened the front door and waved to Emma, who was standing by her car, then turned back to face him. "I've got to go, Nick."

There were tears in her voice, which wrenched at him. Leaning past her, he stuck his head out the door and held up a finger to Emma, who crossed her arms and looked...uneasy?

A friend who rushed to the rescue, yet looked unhappy about it? Not reassuring.

"How did you meet her?" Nick asked Danielle, watching as Emma pulled out a cell phone.

Danielle fiddled with Sadie's collar, looking busy.

He reached for both her arms and made her look at him. "How, Danielle?"

"I met her at a show, okay?" She shrugged free. "That was the one good thing that came out of being with Ted. He introduced me to some really great people."

"Tell her *I'll* take you to Donald's."

"Nick, we already worked this out. If I still need the car after seeing Donald, she's going to let me keep it a little longer."

"Just tell her."

Emma clicked off the cell phone and looked right at Nick.

As a result, the hair stood up on his arms, as it always did when he was onto something in a story he was working on. "Do this for me," he said to Danielle. *And you.*

"Nick—"

Striding past her, he walked right up to Emma. "Good morning," he said politely. "So...where are you two headed?"

Emma glanced at Danielle, who had followed him.

"Emma," she said. "This is Nick Cooper, and—"

"And you're Emma." Nick pinned her with his most intimidating stare. "So...?"

"I'll take Danielle wherever she wants to go," Emma said, smiling at Danielle. "Ready?"

"To the art director's?" Nick pressed.

"Yes, right." Avoiding Nick's gaze entirely now, Emma took Danielle's arm.

Nick grabbed the cell out of Emma's hand and hit redial.

"Hey!"

With a grim smile, he held up the display to Danielle. "Recognize this number?"

Danielle looked at it and paled. "It's Ted's." She turned to Emma. "You just called Ted?"

Emma's smile crumbled, replaced by a fierce concern. "Don't be upset with me, he told me how much you love him, how this is all one big misunderstanding. He truly loves you, too, Danielle. He's devastated by this separation. When he came looking for you, he begged me to contact him the moment I heard anything, so I did. All he wants is to see you, talk to you."

"You told him where I was? Even when I asked for your confidence?"

Emma reached out for her hand. "Danielle—"

"I trusted you. My God," she said on a mirthless laugh, backing up. "When will I learn?" She pointed to Emma's car. "You'd better go."

"Danielle, listen. We're friends."

"*Friends?* Are you kidding? Sadie—"

"It's not the dog I'm worried about," Emma said beseechingly. "Ted said he just wants you back—"

"Wants me back?" Danielle nearly swallowed her tongue. "If he wants me back, Emma, why did he call the police?"

"Well—"

"Tell me you didn't tell him where you were supposed to take me."

"No, not yet—"

"Don't tell him. If you care about me at all, then—"

"Of course I care about you!"

"Then don't tell him."

"Danielle—"

"Please go."

"But—"

"*Now*, Emma."

Nick watched Danielle watch her "friend" drive off. He watched her shoulders sag slightly. Watched while she rubbed her temples, looking defeated and exhausted.

Any moment now she'd catch her breath and momentum. Any moment she'd straighten those shoulders and give him a cool look, the one that would probably work on anyone else, and tell him she had to go, too.

Before she could, he took her hand, and—risking certain death—Sadie's leash. "We're outta here."

"What?" She gave him that cool look he'd been expecting. "There's no we."

"There is now."

# 10

DANIELLE WAS REELING enough to let Nick take over. Enough to watch while he took care of all evidence of her being in his place, including shoving his sheets in the washing machine.

He looked perfectly at home measuring out the detergent. He even dumped the trash, which included, as she knew all too well, three used condoms.

It was only when he came to the two huge land mines in his front yard, left there by Sadie, that he hesitated. Still, he gamely found a shovel and took care of that, too, though he did shoot Sadie several dark looks that the dog freely and openly returned.

Then Nick tossed a duffel bag in the truck bed and backed them out of his driveway. Sadie had gotten into the vehicle docilely enough—probably because Danielle had as well—but now, as Nick drove, she whined.

Danielle felt like doing the same.

After about twenty minutes, Nick pulled up to a

hotel. He turned off the truck and turned to her. Reaching for her hand, he gave her a careful once-over. "You okay?"

"Peachy."

"I take it that's a no."

Danielle closed her eyes. "I just can't believe how stupid I was. I would have let her walk me right into a trap."

"Not stupid. You trusted her."

"I keep forgetting trust isn't an option."

He slid his fingers beneath her hair, massaging the back of her neck until she looked at him. "You can trust me."

"I—" The denial backed up in her throat at the open but fierce expression on his face. "I don't want to trust anyone," she whispered.

"I know," he whispered back, and slowly pulled her against him.

He felt good, solid and warm, and for just a moment she let herself cling. And then somehow she sucked it up, found some desperately needed strength and pulled back. "What are we doing here?"

"Checking in. Then we'll hunt down your Donald and make sure he's on the up-and-up before you approach him."

"Checking in?" She turned forward to face the hotel. "Here?"

"We can't stay at my place."

"*We* can't, no. But you can."

He waited until she looked at him, and his expression was light, neutral almost, but she knew him better now, and didn't miss the determination. "I'm not leaving you alone to face this," he said. "So just forget it."

Why wouldn't he just walk away? Why did he have to sit there looking so good, so right? So...hers? "I can't let you do this, Nick. I don't have enough money for the room, and—"

"It just so happens that I do. I know," he said, putting his fingers over her lips when she would have spoken again. "You don't like help, but you appear to be stuck with me for now." Opening the door, he got out and held out his hand.

She followed, with Sadie in tow. "They might not appreciate Sadie as a guest," she said as they entered the reception area.

"Given that I personally cleaned up after her this morning, I can see why," he said dryly. "But this hotel takes dogs." He pointed to the sign, Dogs Welcome. "Traveling with pets, especially dogs, is pretty common in this area. How many rooms do we need?"

He had the most amazing eyes, she thought inanely, her body tingling in reaction to his unspoken question.

How many rooms? *Just one bed*, her body cried. But her brain was in charge. "We shouldn't get used to—"

"Yeah." And hiding his reaction to that, he turned to the receptionist and reserved two rooms.

AFTER CHECKING IN, Nick drove Danielle to see Donald. When they got there, his office was boarded up, with a sign that announced, We've Moved!

Nick pulled out his cell phone, dialed the new number posted, and handed it over to Danielle, who spoke to the art director's assistant.

When she clicked off the phone, she found Nick watching her very closely.

"Well?"

"I can't see him until tomorrow," she said.

"I heard. What I didn't hear was how you're holding up."

"I'm holding."

His mouth curved. "Good. Now you've got an entire day of vacation ahead of you."

She gaped at him, then laughed. "Vacation?"

"You say that like it's a bad word."

"It's just that I've never really taken one."

"Well, then..." Nick took Sadie's leash in one hand and slipped his other arm around her, starting a lazy walk back to his truck, ignoring the fact that he had to practically drag the reluctant Sadie, who didn't want anyone holding her leash but Danielle. "Stick with me," he said to both unnerved females. "I'll show you how to relax."

But that's what Danielle was afraid of. If she relaxed, she had to let down her guard. And if she let down her guard, he was going to crawl into her heart and make himself right at home.

AT THE HOTEL, Nick waited outside Danielle's door until she slid in the key card and opened her door. "Danielle," he said, and when she turned to look at him, he pressed her against the jamb for a quick, hard, hot kiss.

"What was that for?" she asked a little breathlessly.

He smiled as he trailed a thumb over her bottom lip. "To remind you that even though I'm in another room, you're not alone."

All her life she'd been surrounded by someone

or another, and all her life she'd fought a loneliness she never understood. Now, with just this man for company, she hadn't felt alone once.

"Maybe another kiss would help me remember," she said very softly. "You know, just to be sure."

With a quick, sexy grin, he leaned in, but she put a hand to his chest. "And maybe..." She trailed off.

"Maybe?" he repeated.

"Maybe not so quick this time."

His eyes heated. "Got it." His lips came within a fraction of an inch of hers, then stopped, making her nearly moan out loud. "Is there anything else?" he whispered, his breath mingling with hers. "You know, while I'm here?"

"Well..." He could make her forget anything, including the fact her life had fallen apart. He could make her feel warm and fuzzy and safe by just looking at her. And shameless. He made her shameless. "Maybe just one more thing..."

"Anything." He pulled her against him, letting her feel how hard he was. "You want what you wanted last night? The blinding kisses? The touches that had you trembling?" His voice went rough and low. "How about when I put my tongue—"

"That," she whispered shakily. "That's the one."

"Ah." Eyes gleaming, he dipped his head for a long, messy, glorious kiss that did indeed numb more than half of her brain cells. When he came up for air, he backed her into the room. Kicking it closed, he moved with her until the backs of her legs hit the bed. "I live to provide pleasure," he said wickedly, and pushed her down to the mattress, following her with his long, hard body.

Looping her arms around his neck, she surged up for a kiss, but Nick suddenly went still, then craned his neck to first one side, then the other, looking for something.

"Nick?" She wanted him to take her to oblivion, if only for a little while. "What are you—"

"Sadie?"

*Now* he wanted to talk to her dog? "Nick, I think she can wait—"

"Sadie!" He pushed to his feet, looking around with a startled look on his face. "Where did she go?"

Danielle came up to her elbows. The room was small enough for her to see in one sweeping glance there was no giant dog anywhere. "Oh my God." She leapt to her feet. "She must have walked off when we were in the doorway."

Nick had already hauled open the door again. "Not in the hallway," he said. "I'll go right, you go left."

Danielle ran out the door and turned left, coming to a flight of stairs. *Up or down*, she wondered frantically, then decided down. Sadie would have gone down, it was easier and she was, after all, an incredibly lazy dog.

At the bottom, she pushed open the already ajar door, which led into a courtyard. Bright sunshine had her lifting her hand to block it from her squinting eyes.

Flowers in every color and hue covered every corner. Benches lined the paths, where quite a few people milled around. It looked as if the hotel had hosted a late lunch of some sort, as plenty of well-dressed, important people milled around holding champagne and plates filled with food.

And in the center of the courtyard, in a bed of flowers she'd completely flattened, lay Sadie, her tongue hanging out of her mouth, her coat covered in fresh dirt from the plants, her tail making lazy swipes in that dirt.

Danielle sagged in relief even as she cringed at the damage the dog had done to the flowers, but her relief was short-lived. Because right next to Sadie, tongue also hanging out, tail also swiping lazily in the dirt, lay...another dog.

An even *bigger* dog, who with long, shaggy, dark hair and sheer hugeness had to be none other than a Newfoundland.

When Danielle stopped short at the sight of them, the Newfoundland came to full alert and stood up in front of Sadie.

It didn't take a rocket scientist to see that he was male, and that he'd clearly just claimed Sadie as his own.

In more ways than one.

Nick caught up with her, also stopping short at the sight of Sadie with her new beau, both of whom wore a sleepy, happy, sated expression.

"Well." Nick glanced at Danielle. "I had no idea dogs could look so utterly...laid."

"Oh, no," she groaned. "This can't be happening."

"I take it she's not...er, fixed."

"I was going to eventually breed her! With a *purebred!*"

Sadie's boyfriend sat regally, his tongue hanging out as he panted.

Nick rubbed his jaw, looking like he was fighting a grin. "He looks like a decent enough sort of dog."

Poised and ever so elegant, the male dog lifted his leg and began to lick himself.

Nick laughed.

Danielle groaned, refusing to acknowledge the way the sound of Nick's laugh had the most devastating power to make her want to return it. "This is all your fault!"

"*My* fault!" Now he blinked, looking comically shocked. "How do you figure?"

"You distracted me with that kiss, otherwise I would never have forgotten about Sadie, not even for a second." She stepped into the flowers and grabbed the loose leash at Sadie's side. Then, in a cosmic timing that could only be described as very bad luck, the sprinklers came on.

"Don't say a word," Danielle warned Nick, stepping out of the planter with no dignity and lots of water dripping off her. "Not a single word."

Also dripping water and mud, Sadie shook herself—all over Danielle—then whined, craning her neck to catch one last glimpse of lover boy, her eyes bright and beaming his way.

Lover boy whined in return, and let out one sharp bark.

Nick steered clear of both the dirt and water, looking fit, perfectly dry and...suspiciously amused.

Danielle didn't know if she wanted to smack him, or crane her neck at him and whine, too.

"ARENT YOU WONDERING?" Nick asked as they came to a stop outside their rooms once again.

What she was wondering was, if his voice would ever stop sending a thrilling shiver down her spine. "Wondering...?"

He spoke in her ear. "If she enjoyed him as much as you enjoyed me."

"Step back," she said, still dripping everywhere as she opened her door. "Or I'll make sure you get as hot and wet as I am." His chest brushed her back, his jaw glided along her hair. Simple touch, but oh man, not such a simple reaction, as her knees actually knocked together. "I mean it," she warned.

"Are you really hot and wet?" he asked silkily. "How about creamy? Are you creamy, Danielle?"

Because just the words made her pulse race, she ignored him and hauled Sadie into the bathroom, slamming the door.

Then stared at herself in the reflection, at her glowing skin, at her eyes which were more alive than she'd ever seen them, and took a slow, deep breath.

"It's really a shame he drives me so insane," she told herself. As she could get really, really attached to him.

NICK HAD NEVER BEEN issued a challenge he hadn't faced head-on, and that slammed bathroom door was a challenge if he ever saw one.

Given that, and also that Danielle had just turned on the shower—he sure hated to miss any fun—he reached for the door handle.

Not locked, good sign. He peered around the door to see a still fully dressed Danielle trying to coax a yawning Sadie into the shower.

"Come on," she huffed and puffed as she shoved Sadie from behind. "You're a mess. You've got to... Ugh!" Giving up, she walked around and tried pulling Sadie instead, backing into the spray, closing her eyes as the water hit her full on.

Sadie merely grunted and applied opposite pressure, until with a little screech, Danielle's hands slipped free and she stumbled back against the shower wall.

Sadie escaped.

Still under the spray, Danielle closed her eyes and shook her head.

Grinning, Nick toed off his shoes, and fully dressed, stepped into the shower with Danielle. "Hey, you can wash me. From head to toe, if you'd like." Following up on that promise, he slipped his arms around her and pressed close, thankful that the water currently hitting him in the face was at least nice and warm.

"You're crazy," she said, sounding baffled and grumpy, but she warmed his heart by slipping her arms around his neck. "Completely crazy."

"Yeah." He bent his head and nibbled at her neck. "You taste good." His hands got busy, too, dropping her soaking clothes from her body, eager to be hot, wet flesh to hot, wet flesh.

"Nick." She let out a little sound when he cupped her perfectly curved butt in his hands, gliding her over the unmistakable bulge straining his pants. A sound that suggested she was slightly less grumpy now. "We can't."

His mouth ran over her throat to her bare shoulder, which he gently bit, making her clutch him tight. He liked the way she gripped him, as if she didn't want to ever let go.

"We can't do this in front of Sadie."

"You mean the dog who only a little while ago was doing the same thing?" Nick gestured to the mat on the bathroom floor, where Sadie had passed out on her back, mouth open, eyes closed, snoring away. "Don't think she really cares at the moment. She's exhausted." His hands slid up her body and cupped her breasts, his thumbs rasping over her nipples. "Let's get exhausted, too."

Her misty gray eyes filled with dreaminess and arousal, and she leaned into him, making Nick's heart surge right up into his throat. He wanted that expression on her face permanently, the one that said he was the center of her universe. To make it so, he reined in on the need ripping through him, slowed them both down, dragging out the passion, the hunger, the desperate need until they were panting with it. Only then, when she'd come apart for him, over and over, did he slip into her body and take them both to heaven.

MUCH LATER, Nick ordered them room service. While they waited, Danielle opened her laptop.

Nick hadn't bothered with clothes, and while she waited for her Internet connection, she marveled at how utterly unselfconscious and comfortable in his own skin he looked, studying the room service menu, absently pushing aside a bag of doggie treats on the table.

The bag crinkled, and from a dead sleep on the floor, Sadie came to full attention.

Nick looked at Sadie. Sadie looked at Nick—the two creatures in Danielle's life who'd not yet come to terms.

Nick fingered the snacks.

Sadie stood. Cocked her head. Stared at the treats.

Nick pulled one out, looked it over.

Sadie whined and moved closer.

"So." Nick raised a brow at the dog. "You like me now."

Sadie licked her chops, eyes glued to the treat.

Rolling his eyes, Nick tossed it to her. "You're so easy, dog."

Sadie inhaled the treat, licked her chops and whined again.

And unbelievably, Nick reached back into the bag and tossed her another one.

Danielle felt her insides go still, then sort of melt. Ted had been charming to all dogs. People, too, for that matter. But she suddenly realized it was a fake sort of charming, the kind that never quite reached his eyes. Added to that was the disconcerting fact that he'd cared so deeply what others thought, especially about him.

There was nothing fake about Nick. He was confident, appealing and quite possibly the most easygoing, laid-back man she'd ever met. He didn't care what others thought, of him or anyone else.

Why was that such a turn-on?

She was so busy thinking about this, thinking and staring at Nick's magnificent body as he leaned over the table studying the menu and his selection, that she nearly missed it.

Her Web site had been set up with a bulletin board, so that she could arrange for dog-handling jobs online. She also answered questions and offered advice, and posted the shows she'd be attending.

Among her messages was an anonymous one, and it took her breath.

*You can run, but you can't hide.*

# 11

HAPPILY SATED BY SEX, Nick cruised the room service menu, contemplating how good life felt at the moment. "I could eat everything on here," he said, and when Danielle didn't respond, he looked over his shoulder.

She sat, pale as a ghost, staring at her computer screen.

"Danielle?" He moved toward her. "What's the matter?"

When she only shook her head, he sank to her side and turned her computer so he could read the screen. What he read made his insides cold. "Ted?"

"He thinks I'm running." She closed her eyes. "I *am* running. Damn it." She scrubbed her hands over her face. "I hate this. I hate being on the run, being scared. I'm going to turn this around, Nick. Somehow."

"You will. We will. It's too big to do alone."

"Maybe I can just repay him for whatever he feels she's worth."

Nick knew enough about Ted to know that this problem wasn't going to be resolved that easily. "I don't think money is what he wants."

"You're just saying that because you know I don't have any." She grimaced, then touched his arm. "I'm going to pay you back, Nick, for all you've done. I'll—"

"Now you're going to make me mad," he said mildly. "Look, let's just see what Donald says. If it works out like you hope—"

"It will."

"If it works out," he repeated, "we'll go from there."

"There's that *we* again," she said, her eyes filling with that wariness he was getting damn tired of.

*Get used to it*, he wanted to respond, but as he didn't fully understand the "we" thing himself, he kept quiet.

THEY PULLED UP to Donald's new office, then parked and sat for a moment, studying it.

"Well," Danielle said with false cheer, reaching for the door handle, not wanting Nick to see her nerves, but knowing they were all over her face. "Here I go."

Nick put a hand on her arm. "How did you meet Donald?"

"Uh..." Tired of having made poor choice after poor choice, she hesitated to tell him. "Emma. We were at a show, but I really don't think she'd..."

"Don't you?"

"No," she said firmly, meeting his fathomless gaze. "She thought she was doing the right thing. She really did. She won't interfere again."

Or would she?

Truth was, this industry was small, incestuous in that they all knew one another. It could come out in simple conversation.

"Just be prepared," he said grimly.

They entered the building together. Danielle looked up at the tall, silent, almost unbearably sexy man at her side and marveled that he was there at all. With her.

"What are you thinking?" he asked, putting his hand on the small of her back as if touching her was the most natural thing in the world.

What was she thinking? Only that she'd like him to touch her like that always. "Nothing."

"Uh-huh."

She looked up into a smile that made her stumble.

He tightened his grip until she caught her step. "Thanks," she whispered, squeezing his hand. "But, Nick? Someday I want to be there when you need *me*."

Surprise lit in his eyes, as if no one had ever offered that before. After a long beat he said, "I just might hold you to that."

DONALD WAS STANDING at the receptionist's desk when they walked in. The art director took a look at Sadie, definitely not shocked to see her, then looked up at Danielle.

He was a small, compact man, fit and tanned, wearing an expression tuned to not happy. "Danielle...what a surprise."

But it hadn't been a surprise at all, she thought, taking his proffered hand. "I made an appointment."

"Yes, I was just looking over my schedule." He glanced at his receptionist. "Your name registered when I saw Sadie."

He wasn't thrilled to see her. Uncomfortable

now, she glanced at Nick, who was watching Donald carefully. For a woman who prided herself on her newly-found independence, she didn't question her relief at having him with her. "The last time I saw you," she said, "you mentioned a possible commercial endorsement for Sadie."

"Yes I did." Donald leaned down and roughed up the top of the dog's head, while Sadie glared at him. "But that was before."

"Before?"

Donald looked at Nick, then back to Danielle. "Where's Ted?"

"I don't know," she answered politely, then gestured to the man at her side. "This is Nick Cooper." She watched the two shake hands, sizing each other up. "What did you mean *before?*"

"I don't want to get in the middle."

"The middle?"

"Between you and Ted."

"There is no middle," Danielle said carefully. "This is about Sadie. And me."

"Are you sure about that?"

"Donald, just tell me. Yes or no. Are you interested in working with Sadie?"

"Let's talk in here," he said, and ushered them

into his large, still mostly packed office, holding the door open for them. But as Sadie crossed the threshold, he stopped her. "People only," he said pleasantly, reaching for her leash, smiling at Danielle. "She'll be perfectly comfortable out here with Linda, my receptionist."

Before either Danielle or Nick could reply, he'd shut the door, leaving them in the office. Alone.

Danielle bit her lip and looked at the door. "No, that's not right. Something's off."

"I'll say," Nick said, reaching for the handle. "We keep Sadie with us, at all times."

But Sadie wasn't at the reception desk, and neither was Donald.

They were hurrying down a hallway as he punched numbers on his cell phone.

Nick whistled sharply, and unbelievably, Sadie halted in her tracks, craning her neck to look at him.

As her leash tightened, Donald jerked to a stop, the cell phone tumbling from his fingers, bouncing on the tile floor.

His smile was utterly forced, but before he could say a word, Nick scooped up the cell phone. With a look of thorough disgust, he turned to Danielle. "Take a wild guess."

"Same number Emma was calling?"

"Bingo." Nick grabbed Sadie's leash and handed it to Danielle. "Here's your prize. One dog, free for life. Or until she kills you, whichever comes first."

THE PHONE RANG and Ted held it tight, certain it was *the call.* The one that would bring Danielle back to him.

"I didn't want to get in the middle of this," came Donald's voice. "How did I get in the damn middle, Ted?"

"Money. It changed your mind quick enough. Now what's up?"

"She's with a Nick Cooper. I realize you wanted to know, but I feel funny telling you. As if I'm spying on Danielle."

*Yeah, yeah.*

"They had the dog with them," Donald continued reluctantly. "Look, Ted, I—"

"Thank you," Ted said politely and hung up. Fury blinded him.

She'd left him, she'd really left him.

But it would be okay. He knew where Danielle would go next. She'd want the records only Sadie's breeder could give her. The records that would possibly clear her.

Still, the cold rage ignited, flamed. She wouldn't need clearing if she'd only come back. To him. He was tired of losing things. His house. His wealth.

Respect.

And with that thought, he pitched the phone across the room.

DANIELLE AND NICK DROVE back to the hotel in grim silence. Nick's hands gripped the wheel with force, his expression edgy and dangerous.

No doubt, Danielle figured, he felt good and stuck with her.

What was she going to do? The only thing she knew was dogs, and while she was the best of the best of dog handlers, it didn't matter. Even if she was somehow cleared of theft, the damage had been done. No one in their right mind would hire her now.

And how she'd managed to wrap up the most amazing, most gorgeous, most sexy man in the world in this mess with her was beyond her. She'd barged into his life, let him help her, protect her. Take care of her.

So much for self-sufficiency.

*That* was going to change.

"I'm turning myself in," she said quietly as he pulled into the hotel and shut off the engine.

"Over my dead body," he said, so gently, so kindly, it didn't sink in at first.

"It's my decision, Nick. This can't go on."

Pulling out the keys, he turned to her, his eyes shockingly full of protectiveness, belying that easygoing, almost lazy voice. "You're right," he said. "It can't go on. Do you have a plan?"

"Not yet," she admitted, hating that she didn't. "But I can—"

"*We* can. Whatever it is, *we* can."

Her heart stuttered. She wasn't ready to accept a "we," but having him there at her side had made her feel safe, secure. Two things sorely missing in her life. "You have your own life to get back to. You can't keep doing this with me forever."

"No one can do this forever."

"Nick—"

"I'm not going to walk away, Danielle. Not until you're okay. Don't ask me to."

"I have to."

His eyes were dark. "Is that what you want?"

"I'm sure we both want that."

"Don't speak for me," he said with his first hint

of temper. "I'm asking you. Is that what you really want?"

"Yes," she whispered, then covered her eyes. "Yes. God." She looked at him again. He'd been so quick to mask his surprise and hurt, she wasn't sure she'd even seen it. "It's for the best, Nick, for you to go back to your life."

"I never did like what was best for me," he said, and just like that something inside her warmed. "You realize Ted knows you're here, in the area."

"Yes." She was trying not to panic, not to look over her shoulder at every little sound.

"Let's check out of the hotel, then find another place to go while we figure out what to do."

"That's a lot of 'we' stuff."

"Yeah." His eyes dared her to say more, and suddenly, she didn't want to.

What she *did* want no longer shocked her. "Actually," she said with a catch in her voice, "there are some pretty good uses for the word 'we.'"

His brow raised, and he sent her that slow, sure, sexy smile that never failed to melt her as his strong, warm arms came around her. "Such as...?" His mouth nuzzled her ear, and light-headed already, she tipped her head to the side to give him more room.

"Such as this," she practically purred. "This is good 'we' stuff."

"Mmm." His fingers danced up her ribs. "So the 'we' is working for you?"

"At the moment..." Good Lord, his mouth. "Only because I like the way you kiss," she warned breathlessly.

Against her skin, he grinned. "I can live with that."

"Just so you know..." She broke off with a moan as he'd found a spot on her collarbone that made her writhe. "Soon as I'm done letting you kiss me, I'm done with the 'we.'"

Laughing, he pulled her even closer. "Give it your best shot, sweetheart. Give it your best shot."

"SO WHAT'S THE PLAN? Drive as far as the tank will take us?"

Nick smiled as he drove. "You're a planner. I didn't know that about you."

"You don't know a lot about me." Danielle smiled back at him from the passenger seat of his truck, though he knew her well enough now to see past the dazzling beauty to the nerves shimmering beneath.

What was it about her that made him want to soothe? Protect? He put a hand on her knee, needing the contact in a way that no longer surprised him. "Which reminds me, I'd like to know more about you."

"Other than I'm a wanted woman?"

Her quip didn't fool him. She was scared and unsettled and it infuriated him that her life had come to this. "What have you been doing since high school?" he asked, thinking to distract her. Hell, if she opened up to him in the process, so much the better. "Other than handling dogs, that is. College? Travel? What?"

"No college." She looked out the window. "No money for that, and my grades weren't the greatest. I had a hard time keeping up with schoolwork, with working odd jobs at night."

He'd known that money had been tight and cursed himself for bringing up bad memories. "I'm surprised you stuck around."

She lifted a shoulder. "I've traveled. As a dog handler for the rich and bored, I've taken dogs all over the country to show them, and it's been fun."

"Been?"

She shot him a sad smile that stabbed right into

his heart. "I'm not going to ever be a handler again, not after this."

"Is there something else that would make you as happy?"

She studied the countryside whipping past them. "I'll probably take any job for now, just because I've grown fond of eating."

Nick contemplated that while his gut clenched. He wasn't rich, but he'd never worried about things like having a roof over his head or food in his belly. He'd grown up with few worries and supportive parents who'd seen to it he had the confidence and skills to get through life on his own.

Danielle had the skills, she'd been on her own for far longer than he probably knew or really understood. But how many people had ever believed in her? Encouraged her?

"When I find a permanent place to settle down," she said, "I'd like to save up, go to school." She glanced at him for his reaction. As if maybe she expected him to discourage her. "I'm going to become a veterinarian."

It wasn't hard to smile at that. "You'd make a great vet."

"Yeah?"

"Oh, yeah. You've got the right stuff." His grin widened. "And a great bedside manner."

She grinned back, looking relieved, and with far less nerves than before. "I think I'd make a great vet, too. You could get yourself a dog, you know, and then come see me once in a while for check-ups."

Well, if that didn't bring reality crashing back, he didn't know what did. Soon enough—and if she had her way it would be today—they would part ways.

He'd go back to the job he was no longer certain he wanted, and she would make a new life for herself.

A new life quite far away. Their paths might not cross for another fifteen years.

He didn't like the way his stomach dropped at that thought. "I'm not big on dogs." He glanced at Sadie in the rearview mirror, and oddly enough, felt a twinge at not seeing her again, either.

Oh boy, he was going soft. "When I'm working, I'm on the road. I couldn't have a pet." He felt her studying him intently and wondered what she saw when she looked at him like that. Turning his head he met her gaze. "What?"

"Do you miss your job?"

"Of course," he said automatically, but even as the words left his mouth, they didn't feel right. "I'm not sure," he admitted. "I've been on the go for so long I've forgotten what it was like to slow down and smell the roses."

"You haven't slowed down since I walked in your door."

"True." He laughed. "But even this pace is practically resting compared to how it is when I'm working. To be honest, this relaxing thing, it's...nice."

"What would you do if you weren't racing across the globe for the next story?"

"I don't know."

"Are we having a midlife crisis, Nick?"

"Bite your tongue. I'm not ready for middle age. Besides, I still have two weeks left on vacation to think about it."

"I'm not taking up the rest of your two weeks. Maybe the rest of today..."

"Cooper's Corner," he said suddenly. "It's where I want to take you."

"Where?"

"It's a couple of hours north of here, not too far.

I have a couple of cousins there. They're getting ready to open a bed-and-breakfast."

She frowned. "I was thinking a lot farther away than that."

Yeah, he knew that, but he didn't like the thought of her far away, possibly in another state, completely on her own with no one to turn to.

She bit her lip and considered. "But I do want to go see the woman I got Sadie from. She lives north, too."

"Okay, so we stay in Cooper's Corner while you do that."

"And then I'll go."

And then, from there, she'd go. God, how was he supposed to let her go? "Danielle..." He glanced over before taking his gaze back to the road. "My cousin Maureen, you'll meet her. She used to be a cop."

She stiffened. "Nick—"

"She's good, Danielle."

"No. No cops. Promise you won't tell her."

"Danielle—"

"*Promise*, Nick."

"Fine. I won't tell her until I have to."

"You won't have to."

A muscle in his jaw ticked. He'd never had such an obviously stress-related problem before.

Soon he'd be back to the job. Traveling. Hard news.

And no facial tics.

So why wasn't he happy?

## 12

COOPER'S CORNER WAS nestled in the heart of the rolling hills of the North Berkshires. Just as Nick promised, it was a picturesque rural village, classic New England in character. One main street, lined with tiny, historic shops, mom-and-pop stores and an ice-cream parlor on the corner.

"Mayberry, USA," Danielle said with a smile as they drove through.

"Just don't let the locals hear you say that," Nick warned, giving her a return smile that made her insides turn to mush. "They think they're originals."

Character and charm abounded in the town. The shady old streets were lined with wide, heavy trees that looked as though they'd been there for generations. The sidewalks were rough and bumpy from the gnarled roots of the trees and the antique storefronts were all painted with once bright colors long since faded from exposure. The sun gave everything a glow, and for a moment, Danielle's breath caught as she felt that glow reach all the way to the depths of her soul.

She felt peaceful here. Safe.

But that was silly, she knew nothing about this town, nothing about the people, nothing at all except she wasn't nearly far enough away from her humble beginnings to suit her.

They drove through Cooper's Corner and up a hill, turning into a long, curved driveway where a hanging wood sign beckoned them to Twin Oaks Bed-and-Breakfast.

"This is it," Nick said, taking the last corner.

Ahead lay the inn; a renovated farmhouse, huge and sprawling, surrounded by a magnificent green, hilly setting overlooking the sleepy village below. Danielle just looked at it, her heart in her throat. This was a place to get connected, get grounded. Recharge her batteries. "It's beautiful," she whispered, feeling silly for being so moved.

"My great-uncle, Warren Cooper, built it in 1875. Quite a legacy, these 160 acres."

They'd decided to leave Sadie in the truck until the introductions were over. Getting out, Nick shook his head in wonder, staring up at the house. "I can't believe all they've done to it since I last saw it. It's amazing. You should have seen how run-down the property was just six months ago."

"It's..." *Comfy,* was all she could think.

"Yeah." He slipped his hand in hers, just as the front door opened. A woman came out, shading her eyes with her hand to see them better.

Danielle's heart pounded, her pulse raced. This was it. The beginning of the end. From here she'd go see Laura Lyn, Sadie's breeder, and then it would be over.

Nick would leave.

She'd told herself she'd wanted him to, but she'd lied. Watching him walk away was going to be the most difficult thing she'd ever done.

"Nick!" The woman cried, and, laughing aloud, she ran down the steps and threw herself at him. She was in her early thirties, wearing jeans and a T-shirt, and covered in dried paint of various colors. "Tell me you brought news of civilization, *real* civilization."

"I told you after a week in the boondocks you'd go crazy," Nick said, hugging her. "But admit it, you love it here."

She pulled back and grinned. "I love it here."

"So you're good?"

"I'm better than good." She nodded politely at Danielle. "Hello."

"Maureen," Nick said, reaching to pull Danielle closer. "This is Danielle. My..."

When he didn't finish, Danielle looked at him.

He was looking at her with an unreadable expression that suddenly scared her. Was he going to tell Maureen the truth after he'd promised he wouldn't? No, she didn't really believe that, not for a second, but she did believe there was something wrong because he was looking at her as if he was really, really sorry, and she didn't understand.

"She's my fiancée," Nick said, and Danielle gasped.

He simply grinned as if her reaction was perfectly normal. "She's still not used to hearing it, though. We're here in the Berkshires to surprise her relatives."

With a squeal, Maureen hugged him tight again. Over his cousin's head, Nick looked right at Danielle, who was so shocked a light breeze could have knocked her on her butt.

"Fiancée?" she mouthed.

"I know I didn't call ahead," Nick said to Maureen, eyes locked on Danielle. "We know you're not really quite ready for guests and we've got a big dog, but we were hoping—"

"Of course you can stay here." She pulled back to kiss him full on the mouth. "I'll just go get a room ready! It's still a bit of a mess inside, painting and such, and there are no services yet—"

"No problem," Nick assured her. "We don't need much."

"Oh, Nick! This is so exciting! I can't wait to tell everyone—"

"About that," Nick said quickly, grabbing her before she could run off. "We're sort of hoping to keep it a secret, just for a little bit longer."

Her smile fell. "A secret?"

"*Please?*"

"Really?"

"Really."

She let out a long sigh and gave in. "For you, okay. Just don't make me keep it for long because this is just too good. Engaged! Imagine that." Without warning, she turned and hugged Danielle. "I don't know how you caught him, honey, but I'm so glad."

Well. Danielle stood there, feeling stupid, her arms fluttering uselessly behind Maureen for a moment before she awkwardly hugged her back.

"Welcome to the family!" Maureen said with such warmth Danielle was overcome with regret and guilt, which only multiplied when Maureen went inside.

*"Fiancée?"* she said to Nick in disbelief as they went to get Sadie out of the truck.

"I couldn't figure out how to tell her the truth and keep her out of it. She'd want to help."

"Oh."

"And you don't want help."

"Right." She needed to remember that.

"It won't be for long."

She needed to remember that, too. Promising herself that she would, she locked her weak knees together, wrapped Sadie's leash around her wrist and started forward.

DANIELLE MOVED to the window of the room she and Nick had been given and stared down at the steep, green rolling hills beyond, trying not to think.

One room, one bed.

Wondering how this had happened did her no good. *Nick* had happened to her. By now she'd expected to be on her own, fighting panic, certainly, but well on her way to a new life that included no one and nothing but herself and Sadie.

But she hadn't shaken Nick. Hadn't been able to make herself do it, because hour by hour, minute by minute in his company, laughing, talking, running...it was all an experience she'd never forget. With each passing second, she knew it would only be harder to walk away in the end.

And there would be an end, there was always an end.

But the look on his face as he'd told Maureen they were going to get married... She knew it had only been a story he'd had to tell, but he'd looked so fierce, so protective, so...perfectly content to be claiming her as his.

An act, she reminded herself and her racing heart. An act, and a very good one. Maureen and Clint had been warm and kind. Maureen had insisted she think of herself at home here, offering to share meals, and even her car if Danielle needed it.

Which made her feel even worse. She was betraying their trust by not telling the truth, but she could not reveal the truth.

"I'm sorry about the room situation."

She didn't turn and look at him, the man who'd rescued her more than once now, the man who'd somehow wormed his way into her heart. "I thought you were visiting with your cousins."

"Just reinforcing the story."

"Ah, yes. The story." She felt him come up right behind her, so close she could feel his breath in her hair.

"Maureen knows me well," he said. "She wouldn't have bought me not sleeping with my fiancée."

Danielle swiveled to face him, their bodies not touching, and yet heat shimmered between them just the same.

Did he feel it?

She looked into his dark green eyes, heated and full of affection, and thought maybe he did. She forced a smile. "She sure did look surprised at the engagement part."

Nick's mouth twisted into a wry grin. "Let's just say I've never been one to...inspire commitment."

"I'm sure they'll understand when you leave. We'll tell them you have responsibilities to cover for your sisters, and that I—"

"I'm not leaving, Danielle."

She swallowed hard. "Of course you're leaving. You have to. You'll go back, and I'll just go up the highway to talk to the breeder I got Sadie from, and then..." Her mouth was so dry she couldn't have swallowed to save her life. "And then I'm on my way."

"I want to go with you to the breeder."

"That's not necessary."

"I know." He set one hand on the sill behind her, surrounding her with his body. "You're tough," he said gently. "Resilient and strong. You can handle whatever comes your way, I've seen that. I get that." His other hand slid into her hand. "I'm staying for me, not you. I want to know that it comes out all right for you in the end."

It rarely came out all right for her in the end, but this time...this time, she hoped, would be different. *God, please, let it be different.*

He was looking at her in the way that made her insides tremble, and because she was weakening, she pushed away from him, nearly tripping over the sleeping Sadie.

"How does she sleep like that?" he asked in amazement, looking down at the dog, flat on her back, four paws straight up in the air, mouth open, emitting a soft snore every few seconds. He stepped over the comatose thing and moved through the country-casual room, past the four-poster pine bed to Danielle. "So...when do we leave?"

She searched his gaze, for what, she didn't know. Pity? Regret? Anything that would make it easy for pride to flare, to shove him away.

But he only smiled, patient as ever.

"And after we do this last thing together?" she asked. "Then you'll go? Back to your life?"

"You're in an awful hurry to get rid of me."

"You'll go?"

His smile slowly faded. "If you get your answers, I'll go."

"Okay," she said softly, grabbing her backpack. "Then now is as good a time as any."

LAURA LYN MILLER, of Miller Show Dogs, wasn't home. There was a clipboard attached to her front door for visitors, and given the dates of the notes left for her, she hadn't been home all week.

"She's at a show," Danielle said in a neutral voice that didn't come close to fooling Nick.

She was despondent—he could hear it, he could see it—and for the first time in a very long time, he felt completely helpless.

Because she wanted him to go, damn it, and get the hell out of her way.

But he couldn't walk away from her until he knew she was okay. That after only a handful of days he was afraid there was far more to it than that could be his own private hell.

"All I need are her records," Danielle said, still staring at the front door which wouldn't be opening to her. "Proving I was in Sadie's life from the beginning, with my own money. I paid for most of the vaccinations and food and everything else needed, and since Laura Lyn and I stayed in touch at shows, she could be a witness to that fact."

"She'll be back." Nick took her back to the truck. "And so will we."

Danielle was quiet until they were on the road, heading back to the inn. "She'll be gone another week, if she's on the show circuit that I think she's on. And actually..."

He wasn't going to like this. "And actually?"

"She's not too far from here."

"But Ted might go there looking for you."

"It's likely." Voice tight, she stared out the window.

"So we wait."

"I wait. You can't just hang here for a week."

Right. He had a life.

Cooper's Corner came into view, the pretty little village that never failed to draw him in. Small, personal. Unique. Danielle drew him in, just as this place did, he thought, turning into Twin Oaks B&B.

Danielle got out of the truck before he could come around. "I'm going to take Sadie for a walk in the woods."

Alone. That was crystal clear.

Well, good. He'd practice being alone again, too. He watched her go, watched her hold on to Sadie's leash as if the dog was all she had in the entire world.

*What about me*, he wanted to call after her, but that was pathetic so he headed around to the back of the house, to where he could go be alone and mull. Maybe even talk to Maureen.

He'd asked her to run Ted through the system, discreetly, without explaining why he'd asked such a thing. Nick hoped like hell she came up with something. Anything. If so, combined with the threatening e-mail, Danielle's testimony on how he'd treated Sadie, and anything else he could find, it hopefully would be enough to turn things in Danielle's favor.

Danielle, who was currently walking away from him as fast as she could.

On the back deck, which spread the entire length of the house, sat two young, bubbly, laughing women, whom he recognized as Maureen's clean-ing crew.

They grinned at him. "On a break," the red-headed one called out cheerfully, having unfas-tened all but one button of her sleeveless blouse so that she could tie it between her very generous breasts.

The other had rolled her biking shorts up to nearly pornographic heights, and since she lay on her belly in a lounge, he had an unobstructed view of a very curvy, very nearly exposed bottom. From over her shoulder, she smiled. "Care to join us?"

"Uh..." Definitely, there was something wrong with him that he hesitated, glanced back over his own shoulder for one last sight of Danielle.

But she was long gone.

And damn it, so was any libido he might have had.

That it was possible for her to have so com-pletely stolen all his lustful urges in such a short time was truly terrifying, and he turned back to the women, staring at their bodies, determined to get his own to react.

Not a twinge.

No getting around it. What he wanted, what he

craved, was one slender, sweetly sexy, misty-eyed Danielle.

Only problem was—and here was another first—she didn't want him back.

He knew he had decent looks. That wasn't ego talking, but fact. He also knew he hadn't been bad in bed. The way she'd clutched at him, staring into his eyes with sweet, sexy, wondrous surprise, as if no one had ever made her feel like that before, told him that.

It hadn't been his company, either, because no matter what she pretended, she liked him, he could see it in her eyes, taste it in her kiss.

And whether she wanted to admit it or not, she trusted him. She'd trusted him with the truth, she'd trusted him to be with her. She'd trusted him to help her.

She hadn't let anyone else do any of those things.

But she didn't *want* to trust him. Didn't *want* to let him in.

And without that, they had nothing.

Little Buxom Redhead wriggled on the lounge, getting herself comfortable while watching him from beneath lowered lashes to make sure he was catching it all.

"Sorry, ladies," he said, knowing he was truly

certifiable. But the niggling in the back of his mind had turned to a full instinctive awareness of trouble, and his instincts were never wrong. Without another look at the women, he pivoted and followed Danielle.

She wasn't on the trail. She wasn't in the gardens. She wasn't anywhere.

She was gone.

# 13

DANIELLE GAVE UP the walk in favor of a little ride. Maureen had been so kind, offering her anything she needed, and the fact that she'd taken advantage of that hospitality and borrowed her car felt like an overwhelming burden.

But she still drove herself and Sadie to the dog show to find Laura Lyn.

All the way there Danielle told herself she was doing the right thing, not involving Nick in this any further. He'd done enough, she owed him everything as it was, and...

And who was she fooling?

She'd needed—quite desperately it turned out—to remember what it was like to be on her own, without the incredible, dynamic presence of one Nick Cooper, the only man to ever have her fantasizing about what-ifs.

What-ifs were fruitless. What-ifs were dangerous.

She pulled up to the site of the dog show, taking

a moment to look around at the controlled chaos with a sense of nostalgia. Trailers, campers and minivans dominated the parking lot. Two huge ring tents had been set up for the show itself, and surrounding those were the booths of various vendors selling everything from doggie sweaters to pooper-scoopers.

The hustle and bustle of it, the friendly but stiff competitors, the general craziness had been Danielle's life for so long. It felt like home, and yet oddly enough, also like a dream where she didn't quite belong.

Luckily, it didn't take long to find Laura Lyn, who'd hired Danielle on several occasions to handle her extra dogs. After a quick hello hug, Danielle pulled back and said, "You don't see me standing here."

"Okay." Laura Lyn shifted her perpetual wad of gum from one cheek to the other. "I don't see you standing here—stressed, exhausted and looking like crap. Does that have anything to do with the phone call I took from Ted several days ago?"

Danielle's stomach sank and she gripped Sadie's leash with tense fingers. She looked around, but didn't see him. "This was a bad idea."

"Was it?" Another careful shifting of the gum made Laura Lyn's left cheek bulge. "Why?"

Danielle stopped looking for Ted long enough to look into Laura Lyn's eyes. "I need records."

"Ted said you might. And that I was to call him the moment I saw you." She lifted a brow. "Hard to do that, as I'm not seeing you."

Danielle drew a careful breath. "Laura Lyn..."

"Did you steal Sadie?"

"More like put her in protective custody."

Laura Lyn blew a huge bubble. "Ah."

"I want to show the court that for all intents and purposes, Sadie is mine."

"To prove ownership."

"Right. Then she can stay with me."

"Because Ted broke up with you? Or because Sadie is the most amazing champion the breed has seen in decades?"

So now the story was Ted had broken up with her. Terrific. That gave him even more sympathy in the eyes of the law. "No, not because of any of that." Danielle looked into Laura Lyn's eyes and willed her to understand. "But because Sadie needed to get away from Ted. So did I. Laura Lyn, *I* left *him*. I had good reasons, and now I need to prove Sadie doesn't belong with him." She drew a deep breath and gave it her best shot. "Can you help me do that?"

"*Danielle?*"

Both Danielle and Laura Lyn froze as Laura Lyn's assistant, Gail Winters, came jogging up to them. "Imagine seeing you here," she said to Danielle, with a wealth of speculation in her gaze.

Gail was barely twenty, independently wealthy, gorgeous and far too glamorous for the dog life, but she'd proven herself a good assistant to Laura Lyn.

All that, and she also fancied herself in love with Ted. Given the predatory way she was staring at Danielle, Gail had to know too much.

Under the guise of moving out of the sun, Laura Lyn turned her back to Gail. Then she leaned close to Danielle. "Where should I send the records?"

"That's...complicated."

Laura Lyn looked at her for a long beat. "Gail?" she said over her shoulder. "Could you go brush Max? He's next in the ring."

"But—"

"Now, please, Gail."

Only when her assistant had reluctantly moved away did Laura Lyn speak again. "Complicated?"

"I want to come get them."

"Coming to my place would be a bad idea, Danielle."

"Ted?"

"I think so. How about I overnight the records to you when I get back in a few days?"

Danielle hesitated, because that was a lot of trust, which she was short on at the moment.

"I can have them to you by the end of the week," Laura Lyn promised.

The end of the week. Surely she could wait that long to start her new life. "The Twin Oaks B&B in Cooper's Corner," Danielle said softly.

And hoped she hadn't just made her biggest mistake yet.

DANIELLE DROVE BACK to the inn. Inside, she could hear hammering, the whir of a saw...but saw no one as she climbed the stairs.

Maybe she hadn't been missed.

As she entered her—*their*—room, she removed Sadie's leash, giving the dog space to lie down.

Then Danielle stood still and took her first real breath since she'd left. Maybe Nick had already gone, deciding she was far too much trouble for whatever weak link they had to a past. Maybe he was at this very moment thanking his lucky stars to have gotten rid of her so easily. Maybe he—

"Hey there," he said quietly, and she almost jerked right out of her skin.

Twirling, she saw him, sitting in the chair by the window, legs stretched out in front of him, hands resting on his thighs.

Relaxed and calm.

Except for the sparks shooting out of his eyes.

"I didn't see you," she said with a hand to her racing heart.

"Yeah." He pushed to a stand. "That's a big problem for us."

He was not happy. In fact, he looked fairly furious.

"Nick—"

"You don't see me." He came close so that she could see that it wasn't just anger in those eyes, but something else, something deeper. Fear. Concern. Tension.

All caused by her.

"First," he said, pushing her hair from her face with a surprisingly gentle hand. "Are you all right?"

Was she? Hard to tell with her nerves so highly strung. "Yes."

"Good." He stared at her, then let out a disparaging breath. "Damn it. I'm so mad I forgot what the second thing was."

"Nick—"

"You went to the dog show. Risked yourself. You did it alone because that's the way you wanted it."

"I had to!" she cried. "Nick, I'm going crazy just waiting for things to happen to me. I can't do it anymore. I'm taking control. I'm taking action. I need those records from Laura Lyn, and she's promised to get them to me."

"There's something I need, too, and I'm going to take it now." Then he hauled her up to her toes and kissed her. It tasted of frustration and temper, but more than that, it tasted of affection and need. An intoxicating mix, as she began to understand something she'd missed before. Not some passing fancy, this. Not some vague attempt to bring back their high school days with a cheap thrill.

There was far more to his touch and kiss than that, and she had to admit, far more to hers. "Nick."

"See me, Danielle. Hear me. Stop shutting me out and *feel* me." His hands slid down her back to her hips, binding her to him as the kiss deepened, somehow tender despite its wild demand.

She met and matched his passion, mating her tongue to his, giving him her own affection and need and temper and frustration, as she suddenly couldn't get close enough, feel him enough.

"You wanted me to be gone when you got back," he said, his breath uneven, pulling back to nuzzle at her ear. "You want me gone now."

"Nick..." How to explain when she didn't understand herself? All she knew was that the only place she'd ever felt safe and sound and at home was here, in his arms.

How could that be?

"I know we started fast," he murmured. "But I don't want to finish fast." He slid his hands up her ribs, his thumbs just brushing the undersides of her breasts.

She opened her mouth to say she liked fast, but all that came out was a groan. Encouraged, he moved his hands beneath her top, cupping her breasts, stroking her nipples until she shuddered, pressing shamelessly against him while his mouth feasted on hers. This man...no one had ever touched her like this man. Fascinated, needy, her hands explored him too, slipping beneath his shirt, feeling the muscles in his back hard and tense under her touch.

"I want more," he said, and his fingers slid down her back and dipped under the lace of her panties. She shifted, making access easier, loving the sound that came from his throat when he found her wet for him.

"I can't walk away," he said hoarsely, running his busy mouth down her neck, his hands still in her panties, his hips pressing to hers. "You should know that."

"Yes..." She could hardly stand. "And you should know..." *I'm halfway to orgasm.* "You scare me to death."

At the words, torn from her throat, he took his hands from her and went utterly still.

"Not physically," she added quickly, linking her arms around his neck, pressing even closer. *Don't stop.* "Never physically. But God, Nick..." She managed to look directly into his eyes. "You threaten my heart. Surely you know that."

"I only know you threaten mine."

"That's why this won't work. We—"

"Kiss me, Danielle." His voice was rough with regret, need. "Just shut up and kiss me."

"I can do that." She heard the sound of impending loss in her own voice, too, and tried not to. Her fingers tightened in his hair as she drew his mouth back to hers. Then, when they could no longer breathe, but neither wanted to break away, Nick rested his cheek against her hair. She felt his heart thundering, felt her own matching it.

She could love him.

With so little effort, she could fall good and hard. With a little sigh for what might have been, with a sigh for what might be her last night with him, she let him back her to the bed.

NICK LOST HIMSELF in the moment, concentrating on binding Danielle so tightly to him that for once she wouldn't be able to rebuild that wall around her heart afterward. He was shameless about it, using his lips, his tongue, his teeth, making her tremble and buck and arch beneath him.

"I'm having trouble breathing," she informed him, trying to crawl into his body.

Good. He couldn't breathe, either.

The night had come upon them. The low-burning lamp by the bed made her skin glow, made her eyes soft and dreamy, and he knew he'd never forget how she looked right in that moment, sighing with the pleasure that he gave her. He wanted to overdose her on that pleasure, wanted to keep her pliant and weak with desire.

For him.

They were down to their underwear, kneeling on the bed, mouths clinging. Nick's plan was to make her wild, but she turned the tables and did it to him as she ran her hands over his body.

"You're so beautifully made, Nick."

"Mmm, not like you." Bending his head, he licked the smooth curve that plumped out of her bra, inhaling the warm female scent of her as his fingers slid along her rib cage to the back, unfastening the hook so that her breasts spilled into his waiting hands.

"Still need more," he decided, and stripped away their remaining clothing, easing her down on the bed, coming against her as the sheets shifted beneath them, as the evening breeze drifted in the window and over their skin.

Naked flesh against naked flesh. Moving, touching, holding, tasting in slow, erotic intent, reveling in the mutual delight. Mutual joy.

He definitely found more than he sought. More than he intended, as his senses soared, his soul stirred and his heart opened.

"Nick," she whispered as he slid into her, her voice filled with all the awe he'd already discovered.

"I know." Joined, vulnerable yet strong, he moved. She moved with him, and the passion rose, consumed, taking him unaware, the hunger made all the more poignant by the accompanying fear that this was unique. Theirs.

Forever.

DARKNESS HAD FALLEN outside, but for Ted, that darkness went soul deep.

He stood outside some godforsaken bed-and-breakfast inn called Twin Oaks.

*Hell*, is what he would have called it. He'd seen them. He'd stood outside, cloaked by the night, and watched them embrace through the glass picture window.

Danielle and her new boyfriend. She'd gotten herself a new boyfriend.

She'd be punished for that.

Even the moon had gone to bed while Ted stood there in the woods. Watching. The window went dark.

Which meant right at this moment, somewhere inside there, lay Danielle with another man.

The fury nearly blinded him, but he forced a long, deep breath. Nothing had changed. She would come back to him. She would.

He would make her.

# 14

NICK SLEPT with Danielle that night, and the next, both against his better judgement.

But he was discovering, when it came to Danielle and his emotions, there was little better judgement to be found. They made love, they talked, they laughed.

And continued to play at being engaged for Nick's family.

But though staying had been his own choice, it turned out to be incredibly difficult, because with each passing day he became more and more sure of the one thing Danielle wouldn't want to hear.

They were meant to be together.

One morning, he woke up to an empty bed. When he surged up with a moment of panic, Sadie opened one eye from her perch on the floor and sent him a baleful stare.

"Well, if you're still here, she must be, too," he decided, relaxing.

Without comment, Sadie closed her eye, ignoring him.

But when Danielle came out of the bathroom, fully dressed, Sadie leaped up to be petted.

"Hey," Nick said softly, still prone. "Come back to bed and wake me up."

"You look awake to me."

"I'm having a nightmare. Comfort me."

She reached down and clipped Sadie's leash. "Sadie needs to be walked."

With a sigh at leaving the warm, cozy bed, Nick rose, jammed his legs into his jeans and came up behind her. "How do you do that?" He stroked a finger over the shoulder left bare by her sleeveless sweater.

"She has to go—"

"Love me with all your heart during the night, then in the light of day pull back. Distance yourself."

She went very still. "I don't do any such thing."

"Really?" He turned her to face him, and looked into her cool gray eyes. "You're doing it right now. Working up a temper to avoid the real issue."

"Which is?"

"Us."

"Nick—"

"Why is that, Danielle? Why do you let me in only when I've got you naked and writhing and desperate for me to make you come—"

"I'm never desperate."

She tried to turn away again but he pressed her into the door. "Wanna bet?" he asked silkily, his thumbs brushing the barest of touches on the very undersides of her breasts, a spot he knew by now made her stretch and purr like a stroked cat.

Her eyes fell closed. "That...won't work."

"Uh-huh." He'd heard the helpless hitch in her voice, and made the movement again, this time reaching slightly higher, nearly to her nipples.

At the base of her neck, her pulse raced. He put his mouth there, tasting the spot, and she let out a little whimper.

"This is..." She trailed off to gasp when he dotted hot, wet, openmouthed kisses down her throat.

He lifted her, just enough to press his erection against the V of her shorts.

"Nick...what are you trying to prove?"

He could hardly remember. "Something about making you desperate for me," he muttered, his mouth still full of her flesh.

"I'm...never desperate."

But the words sounded satisfyingly weak when

he ran his hands up the backs of her thighs, spreading them open so he could step between them.

By the sound of her, she could barely get her words together. Good. Neither could he, damn it.

"The records," she managed. "They should come today."

He knew that, he'd wakened up knowing it, just as he knew she'd be out of here when they did arrive.

"This is it," she said. "We shouldn't—"

"Damn right, we shouldn't. But we are." Not wanting to hear all the reasons they were being fools, his mouth covered hers.

He knew the reasons, every one of them. The kiss obliterated it all from his mind the moment she surrendered with a cry and started kissing him back, hot and hard and wet.

He felt a blinding need, an intense stroke of emotion, and heat raced through his body, so that if he didn't take her now, he would die. Then her shorts were gone, his jeans opened. Lifting her higher yet, he surged into her, making them both cry out. He wasn't sure how he could continue to want her this way, this all-powerful, earth-shattering way, but the wanting consumed him.

"Nick..." It was a sob, torn from her throat, telling him she was consumed, too.

"Wrap your legs around my waist...there. Yeah, *there*." Using the door, he thrust into her glorious, giving body, until with another keening cry, she came. Watching her fall apart, shuddering, mindless, his name on her lips, he followed her over the edge.

It was several moments before he could move, but he finally lifted his face from where he'd planted it against her neck.

Danielle's head was thrown back against the door, her eyes closed, and he could feel her limbs still shaking. He would have touched her, but as his own limbs were still trembling like crazy, he was afraid to let go of his two fistfuls of her bottom, or he'd drop her.

Eyes still closed, she squirmed until he loosened his grip, then she reached for the clothes they'd scattered across the room.

Sweater held to her breasts, she turned to him, eyes miserable. "I can't do this anymore."

"This, as in making love?"

"This, as in playing house." She shoved her legs into her shorts. "This pretending to be engaged." She pulled on her sweater, forgetting her bra.

"This..." She gestured to the door that they'd just done it against. *"That."*

Before he could respond, there came a knock at that very door.

"Nick?" Maureen called through the wood. "Honey, Clint and I just opened some champagne with breakfast. A gift from our distributor. Bring your soon-to-be wife down, we'll have a toast."

Nick looked at Danielle, who gave him a long, solemn, sorrowed look that said *see? It's wrong.*

"Give us a minute," Nick said.

Danielle just shook her head.

She didn't want to play the game anymore, but that was okay, because neither did he. And it was time to tell her. He watched her search for a sock and find it. "I want the real thing, Danielle."

The sock fell from her fingers. "You what?"

"I don't want to pretend anymore, either. I want to sleep with you at night, wake up with you wrapped around me. I want to share your life, and have you share mine."

"You're crazy," she whispered.

"Maybe."

"You can't want to share my life. *I* don't want to share my life."

"I love you, Danielle."

Her expression shuttered and she turned away. Walking to the window, she stared down at the gardens, so alive with color. "That's ridiculous. You don't know me."

"I think I do," he said evenly, which was difficult, as she'd cut him deep with her disbelief.

"Okay, then." Danielle's shoulders were stiff. So was her neck. Hell, her entire body felt so tight she was going to crack and fall apart, limb by limb. "*I* don't know *you*."

"Just because you feel like your back is up against the wall," he said, more quietly now, "isn't a reason to lie to me."

She whipped back to face him, a hot retort on her lips, but it died when she saw that while his voice had sounded confident, he was far from sure of himself.

Above all else, his love for her was shining in his eyes. "Oh, Nick."

His jaw tightened. "You're thrilled."

Terrified, more like. How could facing his love be harder than facing Ted's hatred? "We lead very different lives."

"So?"

"So...you've told me yourself, your job takes you far and wide. You're rarely home."

"And I've also told you, I've enjoyed this break. So much that I'm thinking a little lifestyle change wouldn't be a bad thing. I can still write, Danielle, and not vanish for months at a time." His gaze deepened. "If it's permanence you're looking for."

"That's just it. I don't know what I'm looking for." *Liar, liar, pants on fire.*

"Yes, you do. You just don't want to admit it. God forbid you share yourself—"

"I've tried that, thank you very much!"

"Not with me, you haven't." His eyes were hot. "Don't lump me in with him, Danielle."

"It's not that simple."

"I'm tired of beating my head against the wall to get you to trust me. To want me."

"I want you, Nick. That's never been the problem."

"I'd rather have your trust."

Her ribs felt too tight. Her stomach hurt. She needed air, badly. "I don't do trust." She found her shoes, shoved them on.

"You do at night."

Damn it, where was Sadie's leash?

"You trust me when it's dark," he said behind her. "When you can fool yourself into believing it's just sex, it's just comfort, it's just temporary."

The leash was already on Sadie. Grabbing it, she faced Nick, seeing all his anger and hurt, which made her heart clench tighter.

"But it's in the light of day that the challenge comes," he guessed correctly. "Well, guess what, Danielle? I'm not like him, and I'm never going to be. I'm never going to shove you into some mold, force you to do things you don't want to do. I'm not interested in changing you, or asking you to be someone you're not. I want you, just as you are." He put his hand over hers on the door handle. "But I won't have you look at me with that look, the one that says you're wondering how long before I show my true colors, the one that says that no matter how often you let me make love to you, you're still going to hold back a portion of your heart."

"Nick, stop. Please stop." God, she had to think. *Breathe.* She hauled open the door.

Sadie whined, not happy with the tension, and Danielle gave a little tug on the leash. "Come."

Sadie merely ducked her head and used her weight to tug back.

"Running, Danielle?" Nick asked while she played tug-of-war with the dog.

Damn him for not understanding. This wasn't easy for her, it—

With another whine, Sadie sat on Nick's feet.

"You've run before," Nick noted, putting a hand on Sadie's head. "Hasn't worked for you yet. Why don't you take a stand and work this out?"

Danielle glanced down at her dog, who—she couldn't believe it—refused to budge.

"Go ahead," Nick suggested. "Run. Keep on running. Don't let me in. Don't acknowledge how I feel for you. You'll be happier that way. Right?"

What did he know about it? "Come on, Sadie." She stepped outside the room, but Sadie didn't.

"Leave her." Nick's eyes dared her. "If air is all you need."

"You don't even like her."

His eyes roamed over her before he shook his head. "Still not seeing me, I see."

She stared back at him, tough and tense. He thought he loved her. My God. *Loved* her. She couldn't breathe again, and dropping the leash, she ran for the trails.

Alone.

As always, alone.

NICK LOOKED DOWN at Sadie.

From her perch on his feet—which were quickly losing circulation—she shot him a reproachful, hurt look, as if this mess was all his fault.

"Hey, you're the one who decided to stay here," he pointed out.

Sadie butted his stomach with her head, tilting her face up to blink huge, melting eyes at him.

"Oh, no. Don't give me that. I'm second fiddle and I know it. You should have gone with her."

Sadie let out a long sigh. A pathetic sigh. A poor-me sigh.

"Ah hell." He shoved his fingers through his hair and crouched down. "You know I've grown stupidly attached, right? To the both of you?"

Sadie leaned on him, knocking him to his butt on the floor, and something inside him warmed slightly as she crawled into his lap. "Fine mess, huh?" he muttered, trying to be tough but it was hard with a hundred and fifty pounds of dog sitting on him. Giving up, he wrapped his arms around the damn dog—not an easy feat—and gave her a hug.

The big oaf put her head on his shoulder and let out a long strand of drool, right down his back. He hardly noticed. "It's going to be okay," he told her. *Somehow.*

But how? He could still picture the glitter of tears in Danielle's eyes as he told her he loved her.

His love made her nervous.

His heart cracked at that, and a good amount of his temper drained. But for a man who hadn't even imagined his own happily-ever-after, not quite yet, he had a lot of expectations.

Like being loved back.

NICK TOOK SADIE out back. They sat on the large deck overlooking the gardens, and beyond that, the hillside dotted with bike trails. Far below lay an open meadow, filled with green.

It was a beautiful spot, and Nick knew if peace was what Danielle was seeking, she'd find it out there on the trails.

Maureen came outside and sat by him. "Two things," she said in her usual blunt style. "I had a friend at the station run that Ted of yours."

He could tell by the look on her face she'd found something. "And?" he asked.

"Model citizen. Dedicated worker. Always pays his bills, yadda, yadda."

"But? I think I sense a but at the end of that sentence."

"Oh, yeah, there's a but. Several charges of aggravated assault."

"Convicted?"

"Nope. All the charges were eventually dropped.

But if you take those, along with the fact he was quietly released from two different private investing firms over the past five years for the same reason, again no charges filed, you get a different picture of this so-called model citizen. Do you know this hothead?"

"Not personally." A grimness settled over him. "What's the second thing?"

"Did you go trampling through my newly planted veggies against the east wall of the inn?"

"Are you kidding? And risk certain death?" When she didn't smile, he glanced at Sadie, wondering if she could possibly charm Maureen into forgiveness, for Maureen's possessive feelings about her gardens had become well-known. "Are you sure they're people prints?"

"They're not only people prints, they're male prints. Definitely not Clint's though, he wouldn't dare. Plus, they're too big." She narrowed her eyes at his feet.

"Innocent," he swore, lifting his hands. "But who'd want to be peeking in the windows—" *Ah, hell.*

Ted, aggravated assaulter, dog abuser and all-around asshole.

And Danielle was out there somewhere, alone.

# 15

Today, Danielle thought, striding up a trail on a particularly steep hill, trying to release some of the terrible tension that gripped her. The records from Laura Lyn would arrive today.

Then she'd be free to leave. To walk away.

Which was exactly as she wanted.

Mostly.

Oh, damn Nick Cooper anyway, making her yearn and burn for things that she couldn't have.

She'd so carefully schooled herself to be alone, to not depend on or trust another. Yet his love shimmered and glowed like a beacon, tempting her in ways nothing and no one else ever had.

He was so different from the people she'd let into her life. Not temporary. Not selfish. Not out for only himself.

What would it be like to have someone like that in her world? Someone who cared about her hopes and dreams, and was right there by her side while she achieved them?

But what right, she wondered, kicking a rock, did she have to even think about things like romance and love, when her life was in such a mess? She had to fix things first, because only then would she be free to go after what pleased her.

And Nick Cooper pleased her, no doubt about that. She sank to a large rock and put her hands over her suddenly racing heart. If only...

No. No more if onlys. Soon as she got the records, she'd go straight to the police. If things worked in her favor, then soon she could be on the way to the rest of her life.

Whatever and wherever that life may be. She'd start over, make her life work out this time. She'd go to school. She'd become a vet. She'd—

"Danielle."

At the low, unbearably familiar voice, Danielle took a deep breath and turned. It was Nick, of course, looking uncharacteristically ruffled, as if he'd run the entire way from the inn for her, desperate—

Hauling her into his arms, he pressed close. So close she could feel his heart racing.

Or maybe that was hers.

His hands closed over her, stroking, soothing,

though she thought maybe he was comforting himself, which made no sense.

"God." He pressed his face to her neck. "I couldn't find you, I thought—"

"Nick?" Startled by his fierce possessiveness, the way he was holding her as if he'd never expected to see her again, she brought her arms around him as well, thrilling to the way she felt against him.

His hands cupped her head, and he rubbed his cheek to hers, relief and fear still deeply etched in his face. "I have what you need," he said. "I can help you go back."

"The records from Laura Lyn? They came already?" She pulled back with a smile, which slowly faded at the serious intent on his face. "Tell me," she said, heart pounding. "What's the matter?"

"It's not the records." He ran his hands down her arms. "They're not here yet."

"Then...what?" He was looking at her so solemnly, his hands still gripping her arms as if he never wanted to let her go. "Nick, you're scaring me."

"I had Maureen run Ted through the system."

"You what?"

"She found aggravated assault. He was fired

from two different jobs for it. Danielle, this is what you need to give your testimony weight."

"Oh my God." For the first time in as long as she could remember, the fist in her chest loosened a bit. "I was just sitting here, making the decision to go back no matter what. Whatever it takes. Fines. Jail time. I want my life back, no matter what."

His eyes shone fiercely. "Fines we can manage."

That "we" again. Oddly, the fist loosened all the more.

"And you won't go to jail," he said, determined.

"Nick—"

"I love you, Danielle. Remember that." He ran his thumb over her jaw. "I think you love me back."

She couldn't breathe. "I've only known you a week."

"A lifetime," he corrected. "We've lived a lifetime in that week."

"But there are things I don't know about you." She could hear the fear in her voice. "Things you don't know about me."

"I know enough." In a jerky move, he stepped back, breaking her heart. "But apparently you don't."

"I'm sorry, I—"

"Yeah." Expression unreadable now, he said, "there were footprints in Maureen's garden, outside the house. As if someone was watching from the outside."

Danielle stared at him then turned away. "I gave Laura Lyn this address for the records. Another stupid move, huh? I shouldn't have trusted—"

"Danielle." With a sigh, he started to step close again but the radio at his hip crackled. "Maureen insisted I take the two-way." Lifting it to his mouth, he said, "Got her. Safe and sound."

"Good." Maureen's voice filled their little clearing, her worry coming through loud and clear. "You guys have Sadie, right?"

"She's asleep in the garden by the sunflowers."

"No, she's not."

Nick looked at Danielle, his eyes filling with tension as he spoke into the radio. "How about the veggies? Is she there?"

"No." Maureen's voice caught. "Nick, we can't find her anywhere. She's gone."

"We'll be right there." He hooked the radio on his belt and reached for Danielle's hand. "We'll find her."

Danielle thought of Sadie in Ted's hands and

barely felt Nick's fingers in hers. "I failed her after all."

"Not yet, you haven't. This isn't over. Let's go."

Even in her own misery, she was able to detect his, and marvel at it. His feelings for Sadie weren't something he faked. Nor did they have anything to do with how much Sadie was worth, or the awards she could bring. He'd simply fallen in love with the dog. And because he had, he'd do anything to help Sadie, to get her back.

She wondered if the love he claimed he had for her meant the same thing.

Wondered if she could ever be half as sure of it as he was.

FROM THE DECK Nick glanced at Danielle. She stood about twenty feet away from him, facing the steep hills and trails, calling for Sadie. The wind blew her hair back from her face, which had gotten some color from the sun. Her lithe, toned legs were bare, as were her arms.

Nick figured he'd never get tired of looking at her. Wanting her. But the wanting went far deeper than the physical. He craved her voice, her laugh. Her thoughts. And he wanted her to feel the same.

"Oh my God, there she is!" Danielle suddenly cried, pointing.

Sadie came barreling out of nowhere, stopping short at the sight of them, head cocked, as if trying to figure out what the fuss was all about.

But twenty minutes later, inside, she was still panting for air, still drenched in sweat, looking the worse for wear.

Not to mention the rope burn around her neck, where someone had clearly tried to restrain her.

"Bullmastiffs are incredibly strong," Danielle said, inspecting the rope burn. "She could easily snap a tie if she didn't want to be held."

"And someone definitely wanted to hold her." Nick kneeled beside the dog and tried to get a better look. Instead, he got licked from chin to forehead for his efforts.

Danielle was running her hands over Sadie carefully, and when she got to her chest, the dog whined and turned, putting her bottom in Danielle's face. When Danielle persisted, Sadie actually growled.

Nick tried, and got the same reaction, though Sadie added a big, sloppy kiss to soften the sound.

"Oh boy," Danielle whispered.

"What?"

"It's not an injury that she's hiding."

"What is it?"

"Her nipples seem to be tender."

"Um...okay."

Danielle bit her lip and looked at Sadie. Then, covering the dog's ears, she leaned closer to Nick. "I think that's a sign that she's in a very early stage of pregnancy."

"*What?* How will you ever tell?" he asked, looking at Sadie's considerable chest and belly.

"You'll be able to tell soon enough, a dog's gestation period is only two months. But this is going to put Ted over the edge, you know. Her pups, from that rogue mutt in the hotel, will be worthless."

"Hey." Nick covered Sadie's ears himself this time. "Don't let her hear that."

"This isn't a joke," she said, rubbing her cheek to Sadie's. "I don't have enough money to take care of myself, much less puppies. But I can't let anyone know that. I can't let her go back to Ted simply because of money. Look what he did to her neck."

"Yeah, we're going to get a record of that." Nick looked up at Maureen and Clint, both of whom nodded.

"Already called the police," Maureen said, holding up her cell phone. "I reported the footprints, too."

Clint stroked Sadie. "It looks like it's time to take a stand, huh, girl?"

Danielle looked at Nick. "Yes," she said cryptically. "It's time to take a stand."

"And then there's the upcoming wedding," Clint added. "We've got to clear everything up for that."

Danielle's eyes widened as she apparently remembered at the same time as Nick that they were supposed to be engaged.

To each other.

"The wedding." Danielle forced a smile. "Clint, about that—"

Jerking upright, Sadie let out a sharp set of barks, then leaped over the back of the couch to press her huge face up against the window. Continuing to pierce everyone's eardrums with the pitch of her barking, her entire body quivered.

"He's out there," Nick guessed.

"The ex?" Maureen asked.

"Yes." Danielle stood, moved toward Sadie. "But this ends today. It ends now," she said, shrugging off Nick. "I'm going out there to do something I never did before. I'm going to tell him what I think, and how this is going to end. I'm going to take a stand."

"Not alone, you're not," Nick said, firmly pulling her away from the window.

"Nick—"

"Yeah, yeah. You hate the 'we,'" he said, disgusted, not caring that both Maureen and Clint were watching and avidly listening. "Screw that. You're *not* alone, so forget it. After this is over, when it's all said and done, then fine. Go be as you want. Alone. More power to you if you can do it without regret."

"Nick—"

"You'll have your damn life back, and—"

"*Nick.*" Danielle swallowed hard and put her hand on his arm. "I meant we. *We'll* take a stand."

"Is Ted armed?" Maureen asked, while Nick stared at Danielle, unable to process that she'd just said *we.*

"No, he worries about his image." Danielle still held Nick's gaze, as if she was trying to tell him something. "He'd never carry a weapon. He just wants Sadie. We can set a trap, put Sadie out on a lead rope. He'll come, he'll threaten her and I'll have witnesses this time."

She looked around hopefully, appealing last to Nick with those wide, beautiful eyes he could never resist. "You'll see," she said to him. "This will work because the police will believe all of you."

Nick shook his head. "You sound as if you want us to stay back while you face him alone."

"Yes. Exactly."

"No—"

"You'll be right there. Waiting. What can happen?"

*Only anything.* "Danielle—"

"I want to do this," she said firmly. "I'm going to do this. I'm sitting out there with her. We'll wait together, Sadie and I, and then it'll be over."

NICK SAT on the darkened deck watching as dusk turned Danielle and Sadie—alone and vulnerable out in the open—into shadows.

She sat on a bench about twenty feet away, surrounded by the newly planted gardens that were Maureen's pride and joy.

He knew his cousins were just on the other side of the house, watching. Waiting. Helping keep his "fiancée" safe. He knew Danielle wouldn't get hurt, that this had to be done.

Logically he knew all this, but as he watched her cuddle the damn dog he'd grown to love too, he couldn't help but feel it was the beginning of the end.

Soon, it would be over. She'd be safe, and on her own. And he'd be on his own, too.

Good. Great. He could go home and catch up with the meaningless dates he'd planned. He could have one every night if he so chose.

But there was just one he cared about right now and she...

And she was watching a man approach her from the trail below.

# 16

"HELLO, TED," Danielle said as he walked toward her.

The man she'd once looked at with her heart in her eyes lifted an envelope. "Your records. From Laura Lyn."

Danielle's stomach clenched at yet another betrayal. "I see."

"I doubt it." He stopped a good five feet back from Sadie, who hadn't moved but had started a low, very unhappy growl. "Gail Winters helped me out. You remember her, don't you?"

Knowing, as sure as she was of her next breath, that Nick was close by and wouldn't let anything happen to either her or Sadie allowed her to speak calmly. "She always did find you charming."

"You used to."

"*Used to* being the operative words here."

His eyes darkened, not with a sexual heat as Nick's did when he looked at her, but with a dangerous, edgy expression that made her thankful she wasn't really alone.

Odd, but being alone suddenly didn't hold the same appeal anymore. It might never again.

She was safe, even staring down Ted. She felt it to the very depth of her soul. Even more devastating, was the sudden realization that she hadn't felt safe often in her life. But whenever she'd been with Nick, then and now, she'd felt it. She was safe with him and had been since the beginning.

"You're looking well," Ted said silkily.

He was not. She'd always thought of the tall, lean, handsome Ted as cool, captivating and sophisticated. Now, with his wrinkled shirt, dirty pants and muddy shoes, he just seemed like a man who got ugly when he didn't get his way. "I'm not afraid of you," she said, and out of the corner of her eyes saw someone shift their weight on the deck.

Nick.

She knew he'd back her up because he cared. Because he wanted her.

Because he loved her.

She waited for the angst over that, for the mistrust, the fear...but it didn't come. In its place was a yearning she was beginning to recognize and understand.

"You should be afraid," Ted told her. "You're in some heavy legal trouble if you don't do as I want. And what I want is for you to come home. To me."

"To be the trophy girlfriend."

"The wife. I want Sadie, too."

"It won't work, Ted. We're too different. I'm not what you want. You're not what I want. Please, let go. Just let go."

"Letting go isn't an option." His eyes were a little wild, and...desperate? "You and Sadie belong with me."

"I won't marry you." It took every ounce of strength not to shrink away from the burst of rage in his gaze. "I'm not coming back." She put her hand on Sadie's large head. Felt Sadie drool on her foot. "Sadie isn't coming back, either. I know it was you who left the threatening e-mail. Who took all the money out of my account. Who's been spying on us. The police are interested in those things."

"You stole from me."

"I think they'll understand why I did when I explain it all. I should never have run, Ted. I should have faced this, and you, from the beginning."

His eyes narrowed and his mouth tightened.

Signs she now recognized as his uncontrollable temper raising its ugly head. When he stepped forward, she stood, and would have moved in front of Sadie but the dog pressed in front of her instead and faced Ted with her teeth bared.

Ted glared down at her. "Have you forgotten who feeds you, dog?"

"I do," Danielle said quietly, her hand still on Sadie. "Let her go. Let's not fight over her, it's not right."

"What's not right is the way you're not listening. Let's go home," he said in an abrupt change of tactic. "We'll talk. Work this out."

"Another dog would be cheaper, Ted."

He shook his head and took another step toward her. "It's not about the dog. It's about you."

"I don't believe that."

"It's true." Ted closed the gap between them and put a hand on her arm.

Just as Sadie put her mouth around his ankle and chomped down.

With a howl, Ted kicked out.

Danielle reacted without thinking. All she knew was that Ted had aimed toward Sadie's belly, the belly that possibly held puppies. With a fierce shriek, she picked up a potted geranium, stood on the bench for leverage and...dropped it on Ted's head.

The pot cracked, dirt rained down and by the time Ted howled again, all her backup forces had arrived: Clint, Maureen and Nick. And all reached for Ted.

"She attacked me," he yelled, shrinking back. "With a plant! She's crazy, she's going to jail, she's—"

"She's this man's fiancée," Maureen said calmly, standing back while Nick easily restrained him.

"She's a thief! She's a liar!" He fought Nick. "Without me she's nothing but a common slut—"

A clod of dirt found its way into Ted's mouth. "Oops," Nick said mildly, as he held Ted down. "Hate it when that happens."

Spitting dirt, Ted screamed obscenities. Everyone ignored him.

The police came.

The neighbors came.

Maureen served tea and chatted cheerfully, talking up her B&B.

Clint clapped Nick on the back. "A keeper," he said, nodding toward Danielle. "Welcome to the family," he said to Danielle with a kiss on the cheek.

"But..." she started, only to have him walk away to join his sister, Maureen.

"I'll tell them everything in the morning," Nick said quietly, staring down into the mug of tea Maureen had forced on him. "Don't worry about it."

"I do worry about it," she said, her voice trembling. "Because..." With surprise she looked down at her hands, which were shaking. "God. I'm more nervous right now than I was facing Ted."

Nick's coolness vanished, and in a heartbeat he was right there, stroking her jaw, reaching for her hand, fury and worry battling for first place in his eyes but not his voice, which remained gentle. "Probably delayed shock. Let's go. I'm taking you inside."

"No, that's not what I meant." She tried to smile. "I'm nervous because I want to tell you...that is...I need to mention..." She closed her eyes, felt his hands slip around her waist and forced them open again. No more weakness. She wanted to be strong, take a stand for this. "Nick, I don't want you to tell them we're not a couple. That we're not in a relationship."

"You don't think they'll understand? Danielle, I never should have told them that lie, I—"

"No, you don't understand. It came to me earlier, I just had to chew on it."

"Chew on what?"

"Don't you see? I don't want it to all be a lie. I *want* to be tied to you. I *want* to hear you tell me you love me again. I *want* to wear your ring, be your wife."

He went very still, then sank to a chair as if his legs would no longer hold him. "Now *I'm* shaking." He drew in a careful breath. "Did you just propose to me?"

"Yes," she said through a lump in her throat. "Yes, I'm proposing. I love you, Nick Cooper. I want to be your wife, through thick and thin, through your travels and my schooling, through puppies and babies."

He opened his mouth but when nothing came out, he shut it again.

"Forever," she added, thinking maybe he didn't quite understand.

He nodded. "Forever."

"Nick?"

"I'm just...I thought you'd want to take off, that maybe we'd see each other once in a while if I asked you just right. I thought—I never imagined..."

"I was that bad? Oh, Nick." She hugged him hard. "I'm sorry I was so slow."

"No, it's okay." His eyes looked suspiciously damp in the light of the moon as he buried his face in her hair.

She squeezed him close, this big, tough, wonderful man who was all hers. "I love you, Nick. I mean it."

"You'd better. I love you back. God, I love you back."

So relieved she could hardly breathe, she pulled back and gave him a stupid grin. "And the rest? How do you feel about the rest?"

"Oh yeah, I want the thick and thin, the travels and schooling, the puppies. The babies. Especially the babies." He kissed her, long and hard. "I want it all. With you."

Sadie pushed between them and whined.

Danielle ran a hand over her huge head. "What's the matter?"

"I think she's lonely," Nick said. "She needs love, too. We'll have to find just the right dog, just for her."

Danielle curled her arms back around Nick, with Sadie pressed between them. "Yes," she murmured, pressing her lips to his. "No one should be alone. Not when they can have this. A mate for life.''

''A mate for life,'' Nick agreed and turned her toward the inn. ''Let's go home.''

''Where's home?''

''Wherever you are. You're going back to school, right?''

''I'd like to.''

''Then we'll go to where the school is. After that...'' He lifted a shoulder. ''Big city, back here, somewhere new...doesn't matter. As long as I'm with you, I'm open.''

''It just happens that so am I.'' She smiled. ''As long as I'm with you.''

*Welcome to Twin Oaks—the new
B&B in Cooper's Corner,
Massachusetts.
Bed and breakfast will
never be the same!*
COOPER'S CORNER, *a new
Harlequin continuity series,
begins August 2002 with*
HIS BROTHER'S BRIDE
*by Tara Taylor Quinn.
Laurel London is staying at Twin
Oaks. So is noted travel writer
William Byrd. Then suddenly, William
vanishes. Policeman Scott Hunter is
on the case and Laurel insists on
being involved. But Scott and Laurel
share a painful history. Can they
mend their heartbreak and get to the
bottom of Byrd's disappearance?
Here's a preview!*

# CHAPTER ONE

SHE WAS STARING out the window. Scott stood in the opening to the gigantic living room at Twin Oaks and sucked in air.

Heart pounding, he couldn't move. Just stared.

She had her back to him, but that didn't matter. He knew her silhouette front, back and sideways. Recognized the way she held her shoulders completely straight, her neck stiff. This meant she was trying to figure something out—or to remember something.

But even if he hadn't paid undue attention to things that weren't his business, he'd still have known it was her.

Laurel. Here. Close again.

Scott was stunned. He'd dreamed Laurel London into Cooper's Corner a million times, even as he'd fully accepted that he was never going to see her again. He could hardly believe it.

He opened his mouth to speak, to call out to her—and had nothing to say.

How did a man calmly say hello to a woman whose heart he'd broken? Whose dreams he'd shattered with the horrible news he'd given her? How did he call out to her, remembering that she'd made it clear she wanted nothing to do with him, that seeing him was too painful to her?

Laurel turned and found him staring at her.

"Scott?" The word was both a whisper and a cry.

He nodded, needing to hold out his arms to her, to crush her to him and promise her that somehow he'd make amends, make things right for her.

But he couldn't.

There were some things a man just couldn't do.

Laurel ran over and threw her arms around his neck, embracing him completely. In the next second she was crying, sobs wracking her body. Tears burned the back of his eyes as they shared a pain too deep to put into any kind of words.

No matter what else had come between them, what wrong he'd been guilty of, they'd both loved Paul fiercely.

Scott's older brother had been the kind of man who instilled such love in those he cared about. For both of them, the loss of Paul meant that life would never be the same again.

After long moments consumed by grief, Laurel pulled back from Scott.

"I'm sorry," she said almost awkwardly. "I guess this weekend has been harder than I thought."

"You've been in town all weekend?"

He didn't know why that thought was just striking him now. Or why the fact that she hadn't contacted him was so painful.

She'd had no reason to contact him. And every reason not to.

"I came to say goodbye," she said softly. "I need to get on with my life."

Scott couldn't say goodbye because now, more than three years and a whole load of guilt later, he had a very strong suspicion that he loved her still.

*Blaze*

The Trueblood, Texas
tradition continues in...

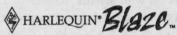

HARLEQUIN® *Blaze*™

**TRULY, MADLY, DEEPLY**
*by Vicki Lewis Thompson*
**August 2002**

Ten years ago Dustin Ramsey and Erica Mann shared their first sexual experience. It was a disaster. Now Dustin's determined to find—and seduce—Erica again, determined to prove to her, and himself, that he can do better. Much, *much* better. Only, little does he guess that Erica's got the same agenda....

*Don't miss Blaze's next two sizzling Trueblood tales,
written by fan favorites Tori Carrington and Debbi Rawlins.
Available at your nearest bookstore
in September and October 2002.*

**TRUEBLOOD, TEXAS**

HARLEQUIN®
*Makes any time special*®

Get ready to enjoy small-town charm
with monthly visits to

C O O P E R ' S   C O R N E R

the town that's the home of the Twin Oaks B&B.
People flock to Cooper's Corner year round to
experience beautiful scenery, warm hospitality...
and some unexpected romantic surprises!

Here's your chance to save $1.00 off the
purchase of HIS BROTHER'S BRIDE
the first Cooper's Corner title.

# Save $1.00 off
### the purchase of *His Brother's Bride*

Look for HIS BROTHER'S BRIDE by *USA Today*
bestselling author Tara Taylor Quinn in August 2002.

RETAILER: Harlequin Enterprises Ltd. will pay the face value of this coupon plus 8¢ if
submitted by customer for this product only. Any other use constitutes fraud. Coupon
is nonassignable. Void if taxed, prohibited or restricted by law. Consumer must pay any
government taxes. For reimbursement submit coupons and proof of sales to:
Harlequin Enterprises Ltd., P.O. Box 880478, El Paso, TX 88588-0478, U.S.A. Cash
value 1/100¢. Valid in the U.S. only.

**Coupon valid until September 30, 2002.**
**Redeemable at participating retail outlets in the U.S. only.**
**Limit one coupon per purchase.**

108227

5  65373 00076  2      (8100)0 10822

Visit us at www.eHarlequin.com
PHCOUPONUS-CC
© 2001 Harlequin Enterprises Ltd.

HARLEQUIN®
*Makes any time special*®

Get ready to enjoy small-town charm
with monthly visits to

COOPER'S CORNER

the town that's the home of the Twin Oaks B&B.
People flock to Cooper's Corner year round to
experience beautiful scenery, warm hospitality...
and some unexpected romantic surprises!

Here's your chance to save $1.00 off the
purchase of HIS BROTHER'S BRIDE
the first Cooper's Corner title.

Visit us at www.eHarlequin.com
PHCOUPONCAN-CC
© 2001 Harlequin Enterprises Ltd.

HARLEQUIN®
*Makes any time special*®

If you enjoyed what you just read,
then we've got an offer you can't resist!

# Take 2 bestselling love stories FREE!
# Plus get a FREE surprise gift!

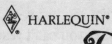

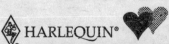